I0731577

Journey to
Mountain of Peace

Patrick O. U. Emerem

Zeta Publishing, Inc
P.O. Box 953
Silver Springs, FL 34489
www.zetapublishing.com

This is a work of fiction. All of the characters, names, incidents, organizations, and dialogue in this novel are either the products of the author's imagination or are used fictitiously.

The views expressed in this work are solely those of the author and do not necessarily reflect the views of the publisher, and the publisher hereby disclaims any responsibility for them.

Ordering Information:
Quantity sales. Special discounts are available on quantity purchases by corporations, associations, and others. For details, contact the publisher at the address above.
Orders by U.S. trade bookstores and wholesalers. Please contact Zeta Publishing: Tel: (352) 694-2553; Fax: (352) 694-1791 or visit www.zetapublishing.com

First published by Xlibris in 2010

Rev. Date: August 8, 2020

ISBN: 978-1-950340-24-8 (sc)
ISBN: 978-1-950340-25-5 (e)

Library of Congress: 2020915675
Printed in the United States of America

Author's Notes

I wish to state that this book was motivated by my first recent international travel to Nigeria, West Africa, in November 2008, and subsequently, in December of 2009. Though this book is a fictional work, some of the imageries were reflections of that travel experience.

It made sense also that I combined this story with characters I learned about in Greek mythology. Thanks to the Internet and the ease of checking things out through Google, especially since it was important to make sure the title was okay and that certain names used does not, indeed, fall into names that I could not use. Furthermore, my favorite author, Rick Riordan, was a source of inspiration.

The idea of this book is to develop four titles to entertain and stimulate the curious minds of general casual readers and to make those readers feel good in the end about the literary work of a young writer. The rest of the four titles and their contexts have been thought out in my head, but I am yet to determine how to write them. The story directions would come once I step in front of computer to type.

It is also expected that this book would encourage young people like me to write using their idle time as my father made me do and as evidenced by this work.

Patrick O. U. Emerem June 2010

To my grandfather Josiah "Ezinna" U. Emerem.

To my grandmother Gladys "Nneihe" Emerem.

To my uncles and aunts for their kind love and affection toward me.

To the elders and members of our family, home village, and those who love peace, harmony, and progress of humankind without inhibitions.

To my father, Mr. O. J. Emerem, for being with me all the time and for doing the first editorial work of this book by checking my spellings, punctuations and questioning my logic and sequence of the parts of the story.

I admired his gentle patience and ability to motivate me at those times it was hard to continue the book. And most importantly, for providing the tools and paying the bills for it's production.

To my mother, Mrs. Catherine C. Emerem for her companionship, support and guidance while I typed my book. Her presence was a great source of encouragement.

To my uncle Pharm. Ernest Onwu for his kind words of support for my schoolwork.

To my teachers at James Martin Middle School and Nathaniel Alexander Elementary School for their hard work at teaching me.

To Ms. Constance Johnson for encouraging and helping to produce my first book Zak's Adventure and Other Stories.

ACKNOWLEDGMENT

I acknowledge that I requested and had my father make major corrections to my initial draft of the Pledge for Peace by Mountain of the End and the bad foreigners, given to Ezinna for the people of Mountain of Peace.

CONTENTS

CHAPTER 1

❈

MY MOM DESTROYS MY BIOLOGY TEACHER

My name is Max Iverson, and I go to Old Government Secondary School, OGSSY, for short. It is a school for really intelligent people.

Am I intelligent?

Yeah, guess you could say that. By the way, I am twelve years old, and I am on a field trip at San Francisco World of Art Museum about Greek Mythology with my history teacher, Mr. Barren. He was the nicest teacher in the whole seventh grade. He was African American and was from Nigeria. He had black hair with white streaks on the side, brown eyes, a gray mustache, and buff shoulders. He likes Greek Mythology, so I thought he'd enjoy the field trip as much as the rest of us.

He talked about monsters, mythical creatures, Titans, and gods. Before I knew it, he was already talking about why and how Titan Lord Kronos swallowed his children so they wouldn't overthrow him; but Zeus, god of sky, destroyed him with his own scythe and sent him to Tartarus and trapped him there forever. Everyone said, "Ill to Kronos for eating his children!"

I wasn't surprised, then we moved onto other exhibits. Mr. Barren and I really bonded that day. But something was suspicious about the teachers at the museum. It was almost time to go, but I didn't feel like leaving. Ms. Cunningham, my biology teacher, decided to tag along in case something happened. Ms. Cunningham (Ms. C for short) had a flowerpatterned blouse, tan pants with girl church shoes, brown hair, and rectangular eyeglasses. I'd say she was in her mid-forties. She was the meanest teacher in the seventh grade.

"Five more minutes left!" she yelled.

I said to myself, something was weird about Ms. C. I could feel it. Then I finished and went out to the bus.

I sat at the back of the bus. I was sitting there alone until Ms. C came in. She stared at me the whole time. I know what you might be thinking. She wasn't staring at me in a stalking kind of way. She was staring at me in a killing kind of way. I wasn't scared or curious. I just ignored her the whole ride back. But the more I ignored her, the more she kept looking at me. As we got out of the bus, Ms. C was trying to get me to talk to her, but I was not ready to listen to her. She offered me to go to a camp for really unique, smart children. I wasn't even tempted to talk to that witch. Then I was tired of her following me, so I finally did. I was really excited to go. I told her I needed to tell my mother.

She said, "Think about that offer."

"I'll bear it in mind," I replied.

Then she disappeared in the shadows.

My mom picked me up from school. She was angry about something, but I couldn't put my finger on it. After a long thirty-minute ride back home, I finally asked her what was wrong.

She yelled, "You're failing biology, Max!"

I told her, "What!" in a surprised voice, then I replied, "How come I got a summer camp for really smart people?" I said it in a sassy way. Then I told her about Ms. C giving me an offer to go to a summer camp for the gifted. She suddenly changed her whole expression into a happy, jolly kind of way. Then she gave me a big hug.

The next day, my mom came out of the car with me to discuss more about the camp with my teacher. We finally found my teacher. She gave us a brochure for the camp, and I couldn't wait until it was summer. Four months later, I was preparing to go to the summer camp because there was only one more day of school. On the last day, everybody was having the time of his or her lives. People were dancing, playing, ruining school property, and most of all, having fun.

Since I was the only one out of the whole school who got an offer to the camp this year, everybody would call me a nerd next year (as if I wasn't already called that).

Anyway, who cares? They are all just jealous, am I right?

I didn't want to act up like the rest of them, so my teacher wouldn't change her mind about her offer. My mom picked me up early so I could pack my stuff. The next day, my mom woke me up very early in the morning. I guess it's because the camp was very far away. We got in my mom's new Cadillac Extravaganza. The color of the car was tan. Inside the car were leather seats. It was my first time seeing it. I was too tired to admire it or ask her where she got it.

We were about forty-eight hours from San Francisco, traveling at about sixty miles per hour just trying to cover the 2,905-mile journey from New York. My mom didn't look tired.

When I finally had enough strength, I asked her where she got the car. She said she'd rented the car from a car shop. I didn't argue.

I was surprised that I never fell asleep during the time being because I always fall asleep in the car. My mom made a few stops at the gas station to get gas and coffee. Now we were about twenty-four hours away from the camp in San Francisco.

After a while, I finally fell asleep. I dreamed of my mom battling a fat guy. My mom had gotten a regular knife and stabbed the man, and he blew up into flames. I woke up, then I looked around, and we were already there. The school looked like a regular school. It had white bricks, triangular black roofs, and two windows on each building of the school. I was glad to be somewhere where you can express your intelligence. When we entered the building, it was a wasteland—dusty lockers, empty hallways, and no people. It was lifeless. As we entered farther into the school, my mom and I saw empty gyms and two empty libraries. The school was smaller than you think.

My mom stayed there for almost two hours, and we still didn't find Ms. C.

"Hello," someone said in a suffering voice behind us. It was Ms. C. She had on a red turtleneck and a long black skirt with a bib on her turtleneck with the word Hungry on it.

I asked her, "Where are all the other students?"

"They are running late," she replied.

"Do you have everything?" my mom said.

"Yes," I told her, and then she kissed me and left.

Ms. C asked me, "Do you know how to play chess?"

"Yes, I do," I told her.

"Before we do anything, I'll show you your room and around the school," she said. Maybe Ms. C isn't so bad after all, I said in my mind.

My room was big; the wallpapers for the walls were maroon, it had two sofa chairs, and one wide- screen TV.

Could this day get any better? I told myself.

The only thing missing was a bed. I didn't even care anymore; I just wanted to enjoy my summer. After showing me around the school, we finally had that game of chess. I looked outside, and it was already noon. What I'd noticed was the other kids still hadn't arrived. After I'd beaten Ms. C at chess, I looked out through the two windows from where we were playing and still no sign of other people.

It was time to eat dinner. I went to the dining table. There was nobody. I became lonely at the dining table. There was nothing else, so I ate a hamburger with some fries that were placed on fine chinaware. I drank some water, then orange juice.

There came to me a magical feeling of being taken. I was like in a trance all of a sudden. I then struggled to force myself to look at the clock to check the time. It was already 9:00 pm. It was time to go to sleep. I fell on the floor due to fatigue, but I still struggled between being awake and suddenly sleepy. Before you knew it, I was on the floor, and I felt a blanket. So I grabbed it and used it to cover myself. This was my first time sleeping on the floor with a blanket. It's more comfortable than you would think. Indeed, I just passed out.

Later, while I was deeply asleep, I had a dream about my brother that went missing when I was between nine and ten. He was talking to someone, but there was nobody there. Sitting in front of him was a golden coffin with a clock in the middle of it. He said something about a plan "going good, my lord". Then I felt a gentle touch on my right arm. And I used my left hand to slap my right arm where I was being touched.

Then I went back to my slumber, and I felt another gentle touch, so I woke up. It was Ms. C right there in my face. She asked me if I had a good sleep. I said, "Yeah, I guess."

She said, "You must be bored because other kids have not arrived."

I rubbed my face to clear my eyes and looked at the clock. It was 4:00 am. That was a whopping seven hours, but it felt like thirty minutes. In a very gentle way, Ms. C said to me, "Do you want to look at the stars with me?" I said yes. Then I had a chilly vibration about her motive and also extremely curious about my dream that Ms. C did not know. Before this time, I didn't like Ms. C so much until she offered me to this camp, so I was trying to like her. But now, I was just suspicious.

I didn't complete my sleep that night partly because Ms. C kept me up to look at the stars with her, and I was just restless. After about one hour, Ms. C decided to go to sleep. Then I went back to my room and tried to sleep, but I could not. So I started watching TV.

The other kids still hadn't come. I hadn't seen Ms. C the whole day. For some reason, time passed by quickly, and when I tried to call my mom, it was like the school canceled out my calls. It was already 6:00 pm and nobody anywhere to be seen. I decided to sleep my problems off. It didn't work.

Then I heard a cold, lifeless voice behind me; it was Ms. C again. She had on a silver Greek breastplate, holding two green flaming swords.

I asked her, "What is going on?"

She pounced on and said, "Your death." I didn't want to fight Ms. C She was an old lady, but on the other hand, she wanted to kill me. She threw one of her swords at me, but it seemed as if she was aiming at my arm, and it was too late. One of them had already scratched my forearm. My arms felt heavy, my vision began to blur, and all I could see was darkness.

As I began to awake, I realized I was outside in some kind of battle arena, tied up to a large stick over a coal-burning fire. I was being roasted. I was too weak to ask Ms. C what in the world she was doing. Then out of nowhere, she changed her form into an ugly creature. Her, or should I say, its skin was completely white with terrifying lobsterlike claws and pincers and spiderlike waist down. I asked her, "What are you?" trying to sound confident as if I wasn't scared of her or it.

"I could take the appearance of any mortal I choose," she said in a bloodthirsty baritone voice. "Now I'm going to eat you, half blood, son of the sea god."

I froze, thinking, What is she talking about? I don't even have a father, or do I?

She opened her large mouth, maybe even larger than a shark's. I thought my whole body couldn't fit in her mouth, but I was stupid enough to boast about it.

Then Ms. C said, "Don't worry, demigod, I'll eat you bit by bit, enjoying your power every second."

That's when I realized I was scared, really scared. Before she could start eating my legs, I saw a huge explosion in the middle of the arena with purple smoke surrounding the explosion. When the smoke disappeared, I saw Mom with a golden bronze pocketknife in her hand. I was relieved to see her. But she didn't look scared or terrified as if she'd seen monsters every day. Suddenly, she used the knife and stabbed Ms. C in the stomach, then Ms. C blew up into flames. My mom untied me faster than I could ask her what was going on.

Chapter 2

My Dad Is A God

I began to ask my mom all sorts of questions all at the same time. I asked her, "How did you get here? And how did you kill Ms. C?"

She told me, "Let's go sit at the rock under that tree and talk about it," as if she didn't even hear a word I said.

So we walked toward the big tree, and she said to me, "I can't explain," in a soft tone.

"Tell me what's going on," I said.

"Okay, Max, your dad is Poseidon, and you're a demigod, and it means that one of your parents is a god and the other is mortal."

"Mom, what are you talking about?" I replied. "What?" I said in a very surprised voice.

"I'll explain it to you when we get to Magic School."

"Magic School?" I asked.

My mom pulled out some sort of potion and threw it on the floor. Then all of a sudden, we appeared in some sort of school. We were standing in the middle of a huge pentagon. Then a man walked toward us. He had brown hair and a brown mustache that connected to his sideburns and made a beard kind of like a goatee. He wore a white vest, a purple cap, and had a horse body from the waist down.

He said to my mom, "Ah! You have arrived, Piper Iverson, and your son finally knows he's a half blood, and he has to train at my school to defend himself from any monster or maybe even a Titan lord."

"Mr. Chiron," my mom said, "might you please take good care of my son and train him well."

"Yes, my goddess, your wish is my command," he replied.

Then I interrupted their conversation by saying, "Goddess! My mom is not a goddess".

"Where did you get that?" Mr. Chiron asked.

"Silly little child, you don't even know your own mother was married to Poseidon and she had an option to become a god, but she choose to continue to be a mortal to take care of you. But she is still known as goddess of premonitions."

Then my mom said, "Stop it, Max. If Chiron is going to be your teacher, you need to respect him, Max."

Then I saw a teenager about eighteen years old, blond hair (not long), golden eyes, and wearing a basketball T-shirt with sky blue jeans. It seemed as if he just woke up from sleep. He looked at me as if he knew me and hadn't seen me in a long time, and then, it hit me.

It was my brother, Drake, who went missing two years ago. I looked at him, longing for this day for two years, and I finally saw him after he had gone missing. I gave him a bear hug. I wanted to yell at him for not telling me what had been going on.

Drake patted me on my messy brown hair and said, "I'm sorry if I worried you, Max, but I had to take care of some stuff, plus Mom, Chiron, and I decided to tell you that you're a half blood when a monster decided to attack."

Then I asked him, "Are you a half blood too?"

"Yes. I am your brother. When I ran away two years ago, Chiron found me and told me everything then. He decided to take me to Magic School to train me and teach me all there is to know about magic."

"You ran away, I thought you—"

"It was just a cover-up Mom told you."

Drake explained to me that it was just a regular school, except they would train me and teach me about magic. Chiron showed me around the school and the classes I'd be taking. He also showed me my room and my roommate. My mom got my bags from the school where she'd destroyed Ms. C. I finally told my mom the dream I had about Drake and the golden coffin.

She said it was probably just a normal dream. I asked her, "What dreams aren't normal?"

She chuckled and said, "Premonitions." She also said that even mortals could have premonitions.

She then told me that the dream I had might be real because I inherited her power. Then after a while, Drake and I said our good-byes to our mom. I was so happy to see Drake again. It was as if he never left. Since it was already ten o'clock, I decided to go to bed. Once I walked in the room, it smelled like peaches, air freshener, and the room was neat unlike before. The color of the wall was sky blue and the two bunk beds were clean. I saw a girl on top of one of the bunk beds. She had blond hair, beautiful green eyes, with blue short shorts and a red shirt that said Rock On in small black print. She was working on a laptop that had a small blue triangle in the center. Until she looked up, I didn't realize how beautiful she was.

She said in a calm voice, "You must be the new half blood." I was so drawn to her beauty, I didn't answer. She didn't talk much. All she did was sit there and work on her laptop.

After a few minutes, I fell asleep. I had another dream. This time it felt real. I saw my roommate chained up on a stonewall sweating. People were booing in some sort of an arena similar to the one where I was about to be eaten. I saw myself fighting a Cyclops covered in a Greek robe. I was holding a sword that was celestial bronze. I had scars all over my body, and I could feel how weak I was, even though it was a dream. The Cyclops was amused at how weak I was.

The Cyclops said to me, "If you cannot defeat me, I will kill you and your pathetic friend."

Then I felt a hard, disturbing rub on my arm, and when I opened my eyes, I was in my room, and it was my roommate whose name I did not know yet. I was glad to see her safe me. She grabbed me, and we ran to Chiron's main office, which was very messy.

"Glad to finally have a conversation with the son of Poseidon," he said.

Then he gave me a sword that was celestial silver and looked exactly like the one in my dream. The blade was three feet long; the handle was brown leather. He said, "The metal was used to create most of the gods' weapons, excluding Zeus, and can only kill supernatural beings." Then it transformed into a ballpoint that was silver. He gave it to me, and I left saying thank-you on my way out.

When I went back to my room, I decided to brush my teeth and take a shower. By the time I came out of the shower, I didn't hear a peep out of the students, and I noticed they were gone. I looked everywhere (if that's even possible because the school was huge). Out of nowhere, an arrow from Chiron's office went flying past me and gave me a little cut. Then my roommate came out from Chiron's office saying sorry. That's when I realized she had flung the arrow. She told me that they were having a game of Capture the Flag. I was so curious of where they could play Capture the Flag in school. There was a door made entirely of glass, and we stepped thorough it. Then all of a sudden, we appeared in a garden that was about forty thousand acres and still nobody to be seen.

"Duck!" she yelled, and arrows with fire swooped over our heads. Even though it wasn't the right time to ask her, I did it anyway.

I asked her, "What is your name?"

"Cindy," she replied.

"What are we playing?" I said.

"Obviously, Capture the Flag with no rules or boundaries."

"So you just kill each other?"

"No, it's just a game."

People shot arrows back and forth, and all I had was a stupid close-range sword. At the end of the game, Drake and his team won. The school was awesome. It even had an indoor arena. Later, Cindy and I were called to Chiron's office to discuss something. When we got there, there was an African boysitting beside Chiron. Chiron looked very serious and so did the boy. Chiron introduced the boy, and I knew this much: his name is Jonah, his godly parent is Hephaestus, a major god, and he was a new demigod that we had to go on a mission with. His hair was black; he wore a shirt that said Wealthy and Wise and dark jeans. I would say he was about my age. Chiron told us the mission took place in the underworld, and we had to save powerful half bloods from Hades. I was not only pretty anxious to go on my first mission but also scared because we might end up fighting Hades.

Jonah said, "That sword is more powerful than you think."

"What's the name?" I asked stupidly.

"White Fang," he replied.

Chiron told us to get anything that we needed on our trip. Cindy brought her laptop as usual, and Jonah brought a water bottle, which is strange because we were going to the underworld. Before Chiron used a portal to take us to the mortal world, he gave me a picture of the two half bloods we had to find. Chiron told me the entrance to the underworld. Once we passed through that portal, I felt more ready than ever.

CHAPTER 3

——— ✾ ———

WE ENTER A WORLD OF NO RETURN

When we arrived at a cemetery where we had to find two rocks, Cindy got out her laptop and scanned the area for supernatural sequences, but her laptop didn't seem to work. Then we saw two rocks beside a tombstone that said Ben and Lana Carmine. Then Jonah went over and read the tombstone a little bit closer. "These are the half bloods that we had to save," he muttered.

"That's impossible," Cindy said.

Then Cindy and I went over to look at the tombstone as well, and he was correct. These were the demigods we had to save.

"Chiron said they were in underworld, he didn't say they died and ended up in the underworld," I said in an angry voice.

"We'll have to go inside and figure it out ourselves," Jonah told us in a voice with a lot of pride. Cindy and I didn't disagree.

Suddenly, when Jonah pulled out his knife, it transformed into an electric spear, and he sliced between the rocks as if he actually knew that those were the rocks to the underworld. In a split second, there was a huge black swirling portal in front of us.

Before we stepped into the portal, I asked Jonah, "Where did you get the spear?"

"My knife turns into an electric spear when I want it to," he replied.

I would have said cool, but then he would give me a big lecture on how more important my sword was than his spear.

We all jumped into the portal holding hands, because if we went in not holding hands, we all could end up differently, by ourselves, anywhere in the underworld. Anyhow, once we passed through the portal, all we saw were candle lights and dark pavement. As we walked, I thought about the dream I had about me fighting that Cyclops. Then out of nowhere, we heard an earthquake that we could feel getting louder.

A big black dog came running at a speed of light. "Hellhound!" Cindy cried.

We ran, trying to find an exit, but I realized we'd come from a portal, not a doorway. "Stop!" a loud voice said.

There was a figure in front of us that wore dark grim reaper clothes. I was scared up until the point where he or she was the one that said stop. When I turned, the hellhound was gone.

Jonah drew his knife out and said, "Who are you?"

The person took the hood off, revealing its face. It was a girl. She had light brown hair tied into a ponytail, pale olive skin, and brown eyes full of worry. I took out the picture of the demigods Chiron gave to us. I looked at the picture and compared the two. Just then, I realized she was one of the half bloods we had to find.

She told us her name was Lana.

"May I show the way to Hades and my brother?" she said in a kind and gentle voice.

"How do you know we are looking for you, your brother, and Hades?" I asked suspiciously. She turned and acted as if she didn't hear me.

We walked a long distance up the stairs. I still had my suspicions about who the girl was and how she knew our reason for coming here. The only reason I became suspicious was because I had already met a shape-shifting monster. After about fifty minutes of walking, when we were coming up the last steps, we saw two big doors. Once she walked toward the door, it opened automatically.

Jonah said, "Are you sure this isn't a trap?"

"Dearly, not," she replied.

Once we walked into the doors as well, the room wasn't as dark as the rest of the underworld. It was like an ice palace with ice pillars on each corner. In front of us was a man in black, a robe just like Lana's. His hair was long and black. He also looked old, and he sat in a black throne in the middle of the room. Next to him was a woman who wore a long green dress with no sleeves and black stilettos.

Then I heard a voice in my mind that said, Max, he is Hades. I tried to speak back, and it worked.

The first thing I said in my mind was, Who is this?

The voice said, Jonah.

I looked at Jonah, and he mouthed, "Tell you later."

I looked at Cindy, and she bowed to Hades and said, "It is a pleasure to meet you," in a shaky voice.

He looked at me in distaste and said, "Lana, why have you brought me this boy?" I had a feeling that he was talking about me.

"Max, why have you come here?" he said as if he knew me.

I gripped on White Fang that was in pen form and said, "How do you know me?"

"How can I not know my own nephew?" he said in a cruel tone.

Suddenly, I was being pulled in front of the god of death. He grabbed me by the neck and pulled me up. He was angry now.

"Instead of killing you, I will throw you in the dungeon," he muttered. As I could barely speak, I managed to say, "What did I do to you?"

"Put him down," the woman said.

"Persephone," Hades said, "his father tried to kill my children."

"Carry on," she told him.

I uncapped White Fang and stabbed Hades in the stomach, but it didn't seem to affect him. He slapped the sword out of my hand and said, "What a useless weapon."

He threw me on the ground, which hurt because I was ten feet above the ground.

Walking skeletons came out of the ground, picked me up, and held me in front of my so-called uncle. Hades touched my head with his index finger and the scenery changed. I was in an apartment that didn't look so bad. There were two sofas and a TV that was small, and I saw a man sitting and talking to a woman. I realized the man was Hades and maybe his wife. I also saw two little children, one a girl and the other a boy. The girl was about six and the boy around three. They were having a conversation about Poseidon. I realized that the woman was mortal. She wore a red sweater and black pants with black shoes. She had brown hair and pale olive skin. By also hearing their conversation, I knew they were married and the kids were theirs. Once I looked at the kids, I now knew the children were Lana and her brother.

Hades said, "Carla, we have to hide you and the kids before Poseidon might finally find us and kill you and the kids."

"We can't just leave," Carla replied in a gentle advising way.

Out of nowhere, mist shrouded the apartment. When the mist vanished, I saw my father, Poseidon. He had a short black beard and wore a dark blue robe. His trident appeared in his hand. He tried to zap the kids, but his accuracy wasn't all that good; and instead of hitting the kids, he hit Carla. Then Poseidon disappeared.

Hades held Carla in his hand, and she touched the side of his face and said, "I love you."

"I'll kill you, Poseidon!" he yelled.

Then the vision disappeared. I was now seeing Hades and Persephone in front of me. I'd never met Poseidon before, but I knew he wasn't kind or friendly.

"Now you see how much pain and suffering the other gods cause. That's why I stay here in the underworld with my wife," Hades said in a sympathetic way, which was kind of weird because he is the god of death. Then the skeletons put me down, but all I was worried about was my friends.

"How is it so that the demigods we are looking for are dead?"

I asked Hades.

"They are not dead," he said. "They faked their deaths so no other god could try to hurt them. And they're not going to Magic School if that's what you want."

"Lord Hades, please," Cindy cried, "they have to come."

"That, love, magic isn't going to work on me, daughter of Aphrodite!" he yelled. Then Jonah said he could create anything he wanted.

"Anything," Hades said in a cruel kind of way. "I want you to create a machine that could kick you out of my palace."

Skeletons came out of the ground and took Jonah, Cindy, and me to a jail cell.

Hades appeared out of our cells and said, "Once you enter the underworld, there is no going back."

"What kind of uncle are you!" I yelled stupidly.

He looked at me awkwardly and said, "What kind of uncle? Your father tried to kill his niece and his nephew, and you're asking me what kind of uncle?" he yelled.

I felt a little guilty inside even though I didn't cause him to hate me. Inside, I thought he wasn't such a bad guy. He disappeared, and we had nothing to do or eat, so we knew we were going to die of boredom and hunger; then out of nowhere, the pen was back in my pocket.

Once I realized Hades hadn't recognized Cindy's laptop, I had an idea. I reached for the laptop, but it shocked me.

"Sorry", Cindy said in a calm manner. "But only I can touch the laptop."

Black smoke appeared everywhere, and I could feel the oxygen being sucked away. Now I knew for sure we were going to die. Suddenly, a large figure stood above Cindy, and he took the laptop, and he was gone. But the black smoke still filled up in the cell.

Then a lightning bolt came out of nowhere and struck Jonah. When the smoke disappeared, Jonah was knocked out cold, and there was nothing we could do about it. Then another lightning bolt struck the cell, but thank the gods, it didn't hit anybody.

When the lightning finished, there was a girl standing there. She had black hair, red tank top, light blue jeans, and was about Drake's age. She carried a quiver on her back and had a silver bow that glistened even in the underworld. I quickly uncapped White Fang and slashed her with all my might, but she raised her bow and used it to block, and I destroyed her enchanted silver bow. Cindy grabbed my shoulder and said, "That's one of my friends that helped me—" Then suddenly, she paused.

"She struck Jonah with lightning!" I replied.

"No, it wasn't me," the girl commented.

"Who did?" I asked her.

"My father, Zeus. By the way, my name is Grace, and I am a demigod as well, and I came to aid you on your quest."

"How do we not know you're a monster in disguise?" I asked her. "If I were to be a monster, I would've killed you already."

"She has a point," Cindy said.

"How do we fight Hades?" I asked.

"I distract him long enough for one of you to get the half bloods."

"It's not like he isn't guarding the place," Cindy said optimistically.

"Don't worry, Cindy, I can take them," she told her.

Her bow began to reform as Grace started to break the cell, and I asked her, "What about Jonah?

We can't just leave him here. We can't carry out this mission with a wounded teammate."

"You're right, Max, one—"

Before she could finish her sentence, I interrupted her and said, "How do you know my name?"

"You're my cousin after all," she replied.

Even though it was true, I didn't think about it that way.

We all decided that Cindy should watch Jonah while Grace and I carried out the mission. We walked slowly so nobody could detect us.

"Grab my hand," Grace whispered.

Suddenly, we appeared in Hades' palace.

"How did you do that?" I asked.

"No time to explain," she said.

Persephone noticed us, but she didn't seem to say anything. Once Hades looked up, he saw us but paid more attention to Grace. "My dead and loyal servants, get them!" he said.

Suddenly, skeletons rose out of the ground, but this time, they were prepared for battle.

"No, Father!" Lana yelled.

I uncapped White Fang and dived into one of the skeletons' stomachs, and it fell to dust. The dust reformed back into a skeleton warrior, and it also multiplied. Hades boasted that we should've stayed in the cell and died slowly. Grace got her arrows and shot all of them, but they just kept reforming and multiplying. Out of nowhere, a hole appeared on the ground and swallowed the dead warriors.

"Lana! What have you done?" Hades yelled

"I'm sorry, Father, but you wanted to hurt them, and they are my friends," she said politely. He looked at us, but he didn't look upset, rather relieved.

"If you take my children, will you leave me alone?" he asked.

"Yes," Grace replied.

"Then so be it," he said. "But I have to remove your memory of you knowing that Lana and Ben are my children so they do not get harmed. I also have to remove your memory, my children," he said.

"I totally understand," I said firmly.

"Flattery," he said. "I hate flattery."

Suddenly, I was kind of scared. Then he waved his hand, and I couldn't remember anything. The only thing I could remember was getting the half bloods and Hades trying to stop us, but after a while, he let us go.

"Can you get my friends back to the surface?" I requested. Then they appeared next to me.

"Next time you try to fight me, I'll kill you," he snarled.

Lana led us out of the underworld, and we were back in the mortal world. We stood beneath a big tree by the roadside. We did not know if it was west, east, or north or south because we were still dazed from the underworld.

Chapter 4

My Brother Almost Killed Me

As we leisurely stood by, a black Lexus came toward us, and all of us were too tired to suspect if it was a monster. Once it stopped, a figure came out; it was Chiron, but he didn't have his horse legs. Maybe it was some sort of potion that hid them.

"Have you succeeded in your mission to get the half bloods?" He asked.

"Yes, Master Chiron," Grace said in a pleased-to-meet-you kind of way.

"Grace, my old student, how was your stay in Olympus?" he asked curiously.

"Good," she replied.

"I think it's time to go back to Magic School," Cindy said.

"Everybody, get in the car," Chiron said. We all hopped in the car, and Grace called shotgun. As we drove, I started to feel back at home, and I hadn't even been away that long; but spending all that time in the underworld must've made the time pass by quickly because it was night, exactly the same hour of day we entered the underworld.

We passed a lot of billboards and advertisement kind of stuff.

"Grace, what does Olympus look like?" I asked.

She kept quiet.

"What happened?" Jonah muttered.

"Was he awake now, Grace?" Jonah asked about me.

"How do you know each other?" I said confusingly.

Before he could answer, Chiron said, "We're almost there." We were slowing down in front of a music record store called New York's Hottest Jams. Chiron got out the car and told the rest of us to come out too. The others didn't look as surprised as I was.

"Uh, Chiron aren't we supposed to be going to Magic School?" I asked wearily.

"This is the original entrance to Magic School than using potions and all that magic junk," he said firmly.

Once we entered, I saw a boy that was may be eleven, and he was admiring the music while eating sour cream and onion chips.

Immediately, as he saw Chiron, he threw the chips on the ground and said, "Hello, Master Chiron." He had tan hair that was cut low, green short-sleeved shirt and black pants.

"Let me introduce you," Chiron said generously. "This is Vincent Fletcher, son of Apollo, a professional at archery, Magic School's youngest counselor, and a master at healing wounds. Vincent, this is Max, Ben, Lana, and you already know Cindy and Grace."

Chiron led us the way to the entrance to Magic School and Vincent followed.

It looked the same as before, but now, there were more people. People were walking in different directions to get to their classes. When I turned around, the only one I saw was Jonah.

I asked him again, "How did you talk to me in my mind?"

"Telepathy link," he replied. "But it is too dangerous because if I die, you might die too." I walked away like I didn't hear what he just said and played it cool. Before you knew it, Chiron was already gone.

"Max Iverson, report to Chiron's office," the intercom announced. I walked straight to his office.

Usually, when he calls, you have to go on a mission, and I did not feel like going on another mission. Once I got there, I saw

Vincent and Drake beside Chiron.

"Sit down," Chiron said in a calm voice. "I'm sorry to say, but you have to go on another mission to West Africa, in Nigeria, where you have to ask Ezinna's permission for us to use his estate and ranch to recruit warriors and as a place for healing wounded warriors for the upcoming war."

"Again" I asked, restlessly?

"Sorry, Max, but when you're a half blood, nothing is easy," Chiron said. "Oh, and the mission starts in a week. For the time being, you can relax and have sword lessons from Drake to improve your swordsmanship skill."

When I left the room, I was kind of mad because I just came back from a life-threatening mission. "One more favor?" Chiron asked.

"What is it?" I moaned.

He kindly said, "May you please show the new half bloods around."

"Sure," I said obnoxiously.

I tried to find them, but they were nowhere to be seen. Drake caught up with me and said, "Let's start that training."

"Chiron told me I have to find the half bloods first," I replied.

"I'll see you later, little bro," he said depressingly.

I felt so bad, but I would make it up to him. Suddenly, as I was walking, I felt weary, my eyes felt heavy, and my legs felt like toothpicks walking on quicksand, then I collapsed face-first.

I had another dream likely to be a premonition. This time, I was in another arena, fighting with five Greek warriors, holding spears in their hands, then the dream changed.

Vincent was fighting Drake, and Drake had Vincent on the floor with his sword at Vincent's neck.

Drake yelled, "The plan cannot go wrong!" While Vincent yelled "traitor," still struggling, he managed to pull out an arrow from a quiver on the table and slammed it on Drake's head, and smoke appeared.

Vincent ran while the smoke distracted my brother, but Drake was too quick. Drake caught up to him, grabbed him, and pushed him down on the floor. Drake got out his sword and jammed it into Vincent's neck, then monsters came from the archery class. That's when I woke up, screaming.

I was back at my dorm, and Cindy was standing right over me, looking at me. "What happened?" I asked.

"You collapsed on the floor, and I found you sleeping, so I took you to the bed," she said.

"Thanks," I told her.

I didn't want to tell anybody about my dream, not even Chiron or my mom. I was still tired, but I also didn't feel like staying in bed all day long and have more dreams.

"Do you want to do archery class with me?" somebody said. Once I turned, it was Vincent, standing next to the door.

And he said, "You know you can be good at a lot of things, but—" I interrupted his sentence, and said, "Not interested."

He walked away and went to swordsmen class. I never noticed that this school was not like other schools. Cindy and I were just sitting here and no one was bothering us. I decided to take archery classes with Vincent, so I went to swordsmen class where he had gone. He was fighting somebody in some sort of twig-leaf armor with a flute in his hand. That's when Vincent saw me.

He stopped the battle immediately and asked me what was wrong. "Archery classes," I said desperately.

Before he could answer, a big explosion occurred.

"Everybody go back to your dorms! And, Grace, sound the alarms!" Chiron yelled.

"What's going on?" I asked Vincent.

"No time to explain," he replied.

I ran to my room like Chiron said. When I got there, I left the door open a little so I could peep. I saw Grace and Chiron standing at the gates of Magic School. When I turned, Cindy was more frightened than me. Once I opened the door a bit farther, I saw a dragon, and Grace shot arrows repeatedly, but the dragon didn't even get scratched. Vincent came out of his room with his bow and quiver. He shot an arrow, but that one was different; it made a supersonic sound wave that was so loud, it could be heard in the mortal world that would reach China. It was also an awful sound. It made all the glass in Magic School break. But the dragon only flinched. That's when I decided to help.

I opened the door and closed it in a way so Cindy could be safe. Before I could even get into battle, a big lion pounced on me. It had a lion body, obviously, a human head, and wings. When Vincent saw me, he yelled, "Sphinx!" He grabbed an arrow out of his quiver and launched it at the creature he called a Sphinx. Luckily, it wasn't a sound arrow because once it hit the Sphinx, green fire emerged from the arrow. He came to my aid and helped me up.

"What are you doing!" he yelled. "Do you want to get yourself killed?"

"I just want to help," I told him fiercely. "Now what's going on?"

"Monsters have overcome the magical boundaries, and now they want to destroy Magic School and kill every demigod in here. This is just the beginning of Kronos's reign of complete destruction," he said in a shaky and fearful voice.

I still decided to stay and fight, but sooner or later, we were going to be outnumbered. I was fighting so many monsters, I couldn't describe them all.

Chiron yelled, "Drake, get the Greek fire!" Drake scurried from his room with a catapult launcher. In his hand, he had a plastic bag with melting green meteorites that almost melted through the bag. He quickly placed them on the catapult and pulled a lever, and then the melting green meteorites were launched in the air. Chiron got a potion out of his pocket and threw it on the ground, then Chiron, Grace, Vincent and I were covered with a magical force field. The meteorites busted into green fireballs that spewed all over the dragon. Then the dragon exploded into sparks of fire. There were still more monsters coming from the gates.

"Everybody, cover your ears!" Vincent yelled. He shot an arrow at the magical gates of Magic School. That arrow was louder than the other arrow, much louder. I looked at him with a wondering face as he mouthed, "Ultrasonic arrow." Suddenly, the monsters stopped coming through to Magic School.

"Grace, Vincent, and Drake, find every half blood in the school you can find and teach them all you know," Chiron said quickly.

He galloped all the way back to his office, and I followed him.

Once he noticed I was following him, he turned and said, "We have no time."

"What's going on?" I demanded.

"My father, Kronos, is trying to gain his true form, destroy Magic School, and obliterate Olympus," he said in a rush.

"We're going to have to train every half blood we can because the war is going to happen in four years." I wasn't sure how he knew exactly when the war was going to occur, but I didn't want to ask any more questions. Before I could leave, he said to me, "Don't forget to learn how to perfect your skills with a sword with Drake."

Once I went to Drake's sword class, I stood at the door, watching him talking and showing the other students how to use a sword.

As soon as the class was over, I saw Drake handing Ben a genuine platinum sword. When they were finished, Ben came out happy as ever.

As soon as Drake saw me, he asked, "What's up?"

"Can you teach me how to use a sword real good?" I said, not sounding so desperate.

"Sure," he replied calmly.

I uncapped White Fang, but for the first time, I actually saw my brother's sword. It looked pretty much the same as mine, but the handle was black leather. Instead of him telling me, he actually showed me.

"I'm ready," I murmured.

"Don't say I didn't warn you," he said.

I slashed sideways, but he countered at the speed of light, and I was open for a blow. For some reason, he didn't strike where I'd left my guard down. I didn't realize up until now that we were fighting in such a small area. He had me on a desk, he also slapped my sword out of my hand, and he had the tip of his sword at my neck. That's when the intercom announced, "Everybody, report to the main gymnasium."

Drake showed me the way to the gym. When we got there, Chiron, Grace, and Vincent were standing on a stage, then Chiron asked Drake to join them. Drake went up, and Vincent shot a sonic arrow to get everybody's attention, and it worked. Chiron began to speak.

"There is a spy amongst us, though I'm not accusing anybody," he said innocently. Everybody gasped because they couldn't believe that one of their best friends might be a spy for a monster or Kronos.

Chiron continued to speak to us, "I want to warn all of you this. If you are caught dealing with an outsider, you shall be dealt with. I do not think that anybody could break into the magical shield and magical boundaries of this school without an insider, which is the spy. It's either you're with us or against us. It is there for your best interest to raise your hand right now if you are the spy, or if you know who the spy is."

No one said anything; they just kept quiet.

Chapter 5

Off To West Africa

“Anyway, we must prepare for your flight to Nigeria in West Africa,” Chiron said sharply.

I knew I was one of the people to go on the mission, so I walked out the door and headed straight for my room. When I got there, I saw Cindy and some boy that was probably thirteen, and they seemed to be having a good time. She blushed a few times, and I couldn’t help to say that I was jealous.

When she saw me, she said, “Um, Max, this is Lucas, son of Hermes.” He had curly blond hair, and he also wore a blue shirt, dark jeans, and shoes that had wings at the side. Anyway, I was still mad, and I was going to challenge him to a sword fight. I reached in my pocket to grab White Fang when I noticed it wasn’t there. He stared at me as if he knew what I was looking for.

He smiled, pulled out his arm, and said, “Looking for this?”

“How did you get that!” I yelled.

I was mad and highly curious how he was just standing there and was able to take my sword. Cindy covered her mouth while she laughed. I looked at him fiercely and sneered.

“I’m sorry, but I couldn’t help myself,” he said carelessly.

“Being the son of Hermes, I am a master at theft and extreme speed."

"I don't care how you did it—but I did—I just want to fight you." He tossed my sword, and I caught it.

"No time to battle," Cindy said swiftly.

I looked at him like a jungle cat and told him, "I'll deal with you later."

He eventually left while we were packing our stuff. I packed my toothbrush and some clothes because I didn't think we were going to stay that long. Cindy packed her toothbrush, laptop, some clothes, and shoes that had wings on them.

When Cindy and I were ready, we walked to the main floor and waited for Chiron and our other teammates. We waited for a good five minutes. After those five minutes, Jonah was ready, and he waited with us. That's when Chiron, a boy that looked like a goat, and Vincent walked toward us. The boy had curly brown hair, brown shirt, and jeans that looked as if they had been in the garbage; and under those jeans were goat hooves, a goat tail, and goat horns on his forehead.

"Max, this is my son, Logan. He is a satyr. Logan, this is Max," Chiron introduced. Vincent later came, and we were set to go.

"I forgot to give this to you," Chiron mentioned.

He gave me a portable red mirror, passports with visas already stamped for everybody. But I didn't want to ask what the mirror was for. We left through the original gates, and we appeared in the music studio that was abandoned. Once we walked outside, we saw the Lexus that Chiron picked us up in.

"Ironic," I said. "There is no one to drive us to the airport."

Vincent turned and studied me. Cindy pulled out her laptop and studied something, which made me mad because the rest of us were thinking of a way for someone to drive.

"Got it!" Cindy boasted. "I have learned the process of how to drive by downloading the easy step- by-step driving process."

"So you can drive, right?" I told her.

"Sure," she said, unhappy because no one was really surprised or happy for her.

We all got into the car, and Vincent pulled the car keys from his pocket, and we were set to go. I hadn't noticed it was dark outside. Everywhere was quiet, which was weird because New York is always busy. While we were driving, I thought about my mom, and if I ever died on any mission, I wondered how she would feel. Suddenly, it felt like a roller coaster going two thousand miles per hour.

"Slow down, Cindy!" Vincent yelled.

But the speed was too much for her to hear him. Then a Fiam! Fiam! Fiam! sound was behind us.

When I turned, I saw a police car and a police officer coming after us. "What do we do now?" I said.

"I told you!" Vincent yelled.

Then Cindy applied the brakes and stopped and said, "What are we going to do now?"

It became quiet like sleep quiet, but we were watching attentively. The police officer stepped out from his car and approached us with his hand on his gun.

Once the police officer came close, the first thing he said was, "How old are you?" in a serious voice.

"Um, twenty-one," Cindy stuttered.

"License and registration, please," he said with no emotion.

Vincent was nibbling on his nails because he was scared we might not make it. Cindy opened the pigeonhole and got the license and registration, but it was Chiron's.

"Um! I got to put some lotion on," Cindy said with a worried face.

But I noticed it was a potion, not a lotion. She gave it to him, and once the officer touched the papers, he looked confused.

Then he said, "Might I help you, ma'am?"

"No, thank you," Cindy replied.

"You have a safe trip," the police officer said. My heart was still pounding from us almost getting caught by the police officer.

Then Cindy said, "We are back on the road."

As time passed by, we were already at the airport. Once we got there, we went to get the baggage ticket, which Chiron already paid for from the baggage clerk. The baggage clerk was a chubby man with brown hair and a uniform similar to police officers' uniform. When Vincent got the ticket, the ticket clerk tipped his hat as if he knew what we were going to do. We all went in the JFK International Airport building and had to go to check how heavy our bags were. When we finished, we got to the line and waited.

"Hey, Cindy! Over here," a voice yelled.

Once we all turned, a girl was walking toward us. She had blond hair tied into a long ponytail, green-piercing eyes, and she wore a pink tank top with regular jeans and tennis shoes.

When she reached us, she asked Cindy how she was doing.

She also looked at me with discomfort, and I guessed it was either she didn't know me or she didn't like me.

Then Cindy boasted, "Max, this is Clair Martin, daughter of Athena. She is a long-time friend of Jonah, Vincent, and me. And Clair, this is Max, son of Poseidon."

"I figured," Clair murmured with an upset voice.

Before I could confront Clair on why she's so angry with me and we hardly met, Cindy boasted again and asked her, "Do you want to come on a mission with us, Clair?"

"We can't!" I shouted.

"Let's call Chiron and ask him," Vincent said happily.

"We don't even have a cell phone," I said with a sassy tone.

"Yeah, we do!" he replied.

And then he dug inside my pocket and took the mirror. Even though I had no clue to what he intended to do, I totally forgot about the mirror Chiron had given me.

He yelled at the mirror, saying, "Chiron, I know you're there." Suddenly, a glowing blue light appeared in the mirror, and then Chiron appeared in the mirror.

"What do you need, Vincent?" He asked in a calm voice.

"Max wants to know if Clair has to come with us," Vincent said. Then he put up the mirror and faced it at Clair.

"I'm sure she can be useful in your mission," Chiron replied.

Instead of getting mad, I just let it go and was going to try to get along with her. Then Chiron disappeared from the mirror.

Vincent put the mirror in his pocket.

Then I looked at him and asked him, "How did you do that?"

"Anybody can do it," he said. "It's a mirror message, and that's why Chiron gave you the mirror."

"You're an idiot," Clair said to me.

"What!" I replied.

"Any half blood should know that," she said.

I ignored her even though it was harder than I thought.

The line was quicker than I imagined. In about five minutes, we were already at the security check. The man used a touch light to look throughout papers and passports. When I passed the x-ray scanner, the person looking at the x-rays on the computer looked at me viciously.

When Vincent was done doing his scan, he leaned toward my ear and whispered, "Monster." As soon as I heard him say that, I turned and asked him, "How do you know?"

"Trust me, I know," he replied.

Vincent was the last to pass, and we were almost done.

As soon as I thought we were done, we had to remove our hand luggage and anything metallic. But I didn't have a belt or a watch. That's when I began to think more deeply into what was in my pocket, which was White Fang, and all the stuff in my hand luggage we needed in the mission.

Then Cindy turned at me, and she knew what I was thinking. She waved her hand at the computer that was checking the metal and hand luggage. Suddenly, she almost collapsed, but then I caught her.

Then she opened her eyes, and I asked, "What did you do?"

"Some of my powers make me fatigue."

I then slightly pushed her up so she could continue. Although she was a little bit wobbly, we finished the security check in no time.

The boring part of traveling is you have to wait for your flight, which is irritating for me because I am active most of the time. The waiting room was pretty basic—couches and tables. Cindy was working on her laptop, Vincent was messing with his Game Boy, Jonah was meditating, and Clair was reading a book.

I walked to Clair and said, "Sorry to bother you, but when is the flight?"

"In five hours," she replied.

I went back to the couch and decided to sleep. Once I lay down, I didn't realize how sleepy I was.

Then I closed my eyes, and I fell asleep. Suddenly, I could feel my skin burning on a stick along where I was tied to. I saw an old man with a long red African cap, white pants, and a white top. He was just sitting there, staring at me. Then I knew, I was dreaming about another old man roasting us in a fire in Africa. I could still feel my skin burning, and I couldn't do anything about it.

Out of nowhere, I felt someone shaking my arm, but it was not in the dream. When I woke up, the first thing I saw was Vincent. I was still scared of my dream, but I managed to get over it. I pretended as if I was not shaken, and I did not tell anyone yet about my dream. I was still trying to figure it out. Then I asked him, "What's going on."

"Same monster at the security check," he replied with a shaky tone.

As soon as he said that, I got up as fast as I could. This time the security checker that looked at me viciously had eyes like a cat—one blue, one red.

"What is that thing?" I asked Vincent.

"Ron," he replied sadly. "He is the most upper-level monster we've ever faced."

"Then how come you didn't identify him at the check point?"

"Because he shape-shifted into his true human form," he said.

"Um! Well, can we beat him?" I said with a really worried tone.

"Max, he broke through the magical force field with no problem and nearly destroyed Magic School before," he replied.

I grabbed White Fang, and I uncapped it. When he saw my sword, his eyes widened in fear. I looked at Vincent in confusion.

I ran toward Ron and charged at him. He dodged in an instant. I kept slashing him, but he kept dodging. When I slashed once more, he grabbed my sword and tossed it far to my right side. For some reason, the mortals didn't seem to notice Ron. His piercing eyes paralyzed me in fear.

Then I heard Vincent yell, "Max, no!"

His bow, quiver, and arrows were in his luggage, not his hand luggage, so no one could save me. Then Ron held me up by my throat and said, "I'll kill you."

Jonah ran quickly toward the monster and me. Jonah pulled out his knife, and it transformed into an electric spear, and he threw it like a javelin. Once it hit Ron, it must've shocked with one hundred billion bolts of lightning even though I didn't know how his spear felt, and I didn't want to know how it felt.

"Aaagh!" he yelled.

Then he dropped me on the ground. But he didn't explode or die; he just looked at Jonah and sneered. As soon as he dropped me, I immediately ran back to the waiting room. Then I went to Cindy and asked, "Why can't the mortals see Ron?"

"The magical force field," she said. "The gods created it so mortals can't see any magical-related stuff. Although some mortals can see through the magical force field, it is rare because, most of the time, special events happen."

"Like what kind?" I replied.

"Either they have a chance of becoming a god or giving birth to a demigod." Before I could speak again, the monster had slung Jonah across the room. "Foolish children!" Ron roared.

"Jonah!" Vincent yelled. Vincent ran and came to his aid.

"I'm going to kill you!" Cindy cried.

She ran toward Ron and pounced on like a kangaroo. But she didn't jump ordinarily; she jumped as fast as a cheetah. Then I noticed she wore the winged shoes she'd packed. Then she kicked him on the face. He fell straight on the ground. He got up slowly, then he jumped and scratched her on the arm. The scratch was deep and colored purple. Jonah had the strength to get up and get his spear. As soon as he did, he stabbed Ron in the heart, and he blew up into flames.

As soon as we defeated the monster, we rushed to Cindy to see how she was doing. "Don't worry," Vincent said, "I can heal you."

He put his hands over the wound, and then his hands began to glow bright orange. "Oh no!" he said.

"What happened?" I murmured.

"It won't heal!" he yelled.

"I'm f-fine," Cindy managed to say. "I can still go to Nigeria and carry out the mission with you all." When she said that, Vincent and I helped Cindy up and put her arms around our necks. We then placed her on the couch. She looked terrible, but she managed. I looked at the clock, and we had two hours left. I had nothing to do; I just sat there.

I was curious why the monster had attacked us, so I went and sat by Vincent. "Vincent," I said, "why did the monster attack us in the first place?"

He looked at the ground and began to speak. "The spy working for Kronos must've known that we would be going on this mission, so he tried to delay us by sending out a high-level monster."

"Um, how powerful is this Kronos guy anyway?" I said curiously.

"Very, but he is not yet in his true form, and he will have to take a host for him to use," he replied.

"So how do we stop him?" I said.

"Nobody knows yet," he said firmly.

"Let's call Chiron and check with him on what's going on." He took the mirror out of his pocket and knocked on it as if it were a door.

Then Chiron appeared in the mirror.

"Vincent! What is it now?" he said with a tired voice.

"We just wanted to see how things were going, oh, and Ron came back to life and tried to kill us again!"

"Calm down, Vincent. Now who tried to kill you all?" he said as if he had no idea what Vincent was talking about.

"Ron!" he yelled.

"Kronos's spy must've tried to make you late for the flight by sending out a powerful monster," Chiron said to him. "Well, I'll have to get into this matter later, but for now, complete your mission successfully because it is an important one." Then Chiron disappeared from the mirror.

Vincent looked at me with a worried face and said, "This is bad, very bad! If Kronos's spy manages to bring back Kronos, the world will end in destruction, chaos, and everything bad."

"This guy really is strong," I replied.

Then he looked at me and said, "Yes, really," with an angered tone.

"Flight 28 will now be arriving to depart soon," the speaker announced.

"That's our flight," Clair said happily. Cindy limped, but I came to her aid and put her arm around my neck. Jonah was right behind us, but he didn't look happy.

"Can you take Cindy from here?" I told Vincent.

"Sure," he replied.

I walked backward to meet up with Jonah and asked him what was wrong. He didn't reply.

Then he started to say something. "My village is in trouble, and I have to help it. So like it or not, I cannot go on the mission without you all."

I looked at him and decided that I would help once we get there. We walked a long distance, but I promised myself that I would not fall asleep in the airplane. We finally got to where the airplane was. As we walked up the stairs of the plane, I felt drowsy, but I didn't have more nightmares or premonitions that were bad if I fell asleep.

Cindy and Clair sat next to each other. Vincent was lucky to have his own seat, and Jonah and I sat next to each other. When I sat in that seat, I noticed that I was sleepier than usual, and I thought it's because, ever since I knew I was a half blood or demigod, I never had a break, and this Kronos guy isn't even alive yet.

No, I can't be selfish. I'm going to complete this mission and defeat Kronos, I also told myself. I guess one little nap couldn't hurt me.

Then I closed my eyes, and it went all downhill from there.

Suddenly, I was in the same type of arena as was in my last dream, fighting a Cyclops. And it was the same dream, same Cyclops, and Cindy tied up on the wall; but this time, the dream was clearer. The new thing about my dream was I saw Drake sitting on a chair while I was still struggling to fight. For some reason, he didn't help me. He just sat there, watching me, and grinning a few times. The Cyclops was huge, and he kept smashing the ground, making mini earthquakes, which made it hard for me to fight. I ran, knowing eventually that I was going to be tired, and he was going to catch up. I couldn't focus on making a plan because of his mini earthquakes. When I decided to strike, he knocked me out of the ground with one gigantic hand.

As I was still struggling to get up, Drake chanted these words: "Finish him off! Finish him off."

I was devastated to hear him say that, but I knew this was just a dream, and I knew my brother would never say that. When those words were chanted, the whole crowd started to scream it.

Finish him off! Finish him off! Finish him off!

They chanted as if they were already in the picture. It was not pretty to hear the loud crowd trying to gang up against me.

Then all of a sudden, the Cyclops started to worship himself when he hadn't even defeated me yet.

As I got up, I knew what to do. I ran and stabbed the Cyclops. Once it hit his stomach, it didn't seem to affect him.

He just looked at me in pity and said, "You fool, and you think you can defeat me?"

Then he grabbed me by the neck, held me up, and started choking me. Then he threw me on the floor. Blood trickled down my cheek, and I was too weak to get on my feet. He lifted his arms, and his hands were balled into a fist, then he put them above me.

"No!" Cindy cried.

"Stop," Drake said mercifully. "Before you crush him to bits, kill his little friend that is chained on the stone."

He suddenly stopped and went toward Cindy. I managed to get up, then I charged again at him before he could reach Cindy. But yet again, he knocked me down.

That's when I was mad.

Suddenly, I could feel power within me. I could sense streams of water in the ground. A rumbling sound came beneath the ground. Water gushed out from the ground at jet speed and hit the Cyclops like a mini tsunami, and he was slammed against the wall of the arena. He fell down flat on his face, and you could hear the vibration on the ground. I was shocked to see that happen, but I knew it was me who did it. Being the son of Poseidon, I knew I could do stuff like that, but I never saw myself do it before. It was the first time I ever used my power.

The crowd went crazy and started booing me because I thought they didn't like demigods defeating creatures or monsters. I went to Cindy and tried to remove her chains.

Then somebody yelled, "Hey! Max!" When I turned, it was Drake who made the comment. "You're not leaving here until you are dead!" he yelled.

He jumped off his throne and pulled out his sword. I knew Drake was a master at swordsmanship, and I had no chance of defeating him in a sword fight.

"You think I'm going to fight you by myself, then you're more stupid than I thought." Suddenly, he pulled out a potion from his pocket and threw it at the Cyclops.

"Arrrgh!" Something yelled and roared. I turned, and the Cyclops was revived.

To make matters worse now, I had to fight the Cyclops, and I didn't even know how I beat him the first time. I was too weak to fight. I concentrated on water, but nothing happened.

"You know you can't win," Drake said modestly. I stared at him, fiercely wondering where his weak spots were and how to beat him.

"Cyclops!" Drake demanded. "Kill the girl immediately!"

The Cyclops walked over to Cindy, rolling his eyes at Drake

for being demanding. Then an idea hit me. If I tricked them by telling the Cyclops that Drake wasn't his boss and he's just as good as him, I could distract them long enough to free Cindy and save her from being in harm's way.

"Hey! Cyclops!" I shouted. "Don't let him boss you around, you're just as strong as he is."

"Yeah! You're just a pathetic demigod," the Cyclops said angrily.

Drake's eyes turned with rage, and they began to argue. I knew my plan would work successfully. I jogged over to where Cindy was chained up. It was a matter of time before they heard that the crowd was saying, "It's a trick!"

I hurried to untie Cindy. In about thirty seconds, she was freed.

Suddenly, my dream shifted. It was nighttime, and the moon was shining as bright as the sun. I was standing in front of a pond with a kid. I noticed that the kid was Ben Carmine. He had on a black jacket with his hood on his head. We were talking about someone having an invasion of some sort, but I couldn't hear the conversation clearly. He brought out his sword, but something was different about it. The sword was sheared, and the color was brownish black.

"Someone is near," he said quietly.

"How can you tell?" I said. He didn't reply. Suddenly, gray wings sprouted from the bush near the tree, then a demonic figure rose above us. It had gray skin, purple lips, fangs, a black reversed X in the middle of its face, and long purple hair. He wore black pants, and his eyes were red.

"It's Wyatt," he said, not surprised.

Then with intense speed, he instantly appeared in front of me and sliced me in half, but it was a water clone. Wondering how I did it, I had no clue, but anyway, I knew he was too strong for Ben and me. Now I knew it was a boy. Instead of Ben to run when he had the courage and ignorance to stick and fight, he stood there with his sword in front of him in battle position. His eyes glared at Wyatt dashingly.

Then Wyatt's wings began to flap down, his whole demonic form slowly began to disintegrate. In his human form, he had a small brown beard, small brown mustache, and a palm-brown hair that reached to his shoulders.

He slowly walked toward Ben, and then he lifted him up by the throat and said, "Son of Hades, you cease to impress me, and for that, I will kill you as quickly as possible."

He turned his head and looked at me and said, "Good job with the water clone, son of Poseidon, but when I'm finished with him, you're next."

Suddenly, my eyes started to glow blue, and I levitated, then the earth began to rumble. Earthquakes started to circulate and water began to make whirlpools the size of the Pacific Ocean. Wyatt's and Ben's eyes widened with amazement. I was surprised too. Suddenly, I knew that the world was at the palm of my hand. Wyatt transformed into his demonic form and dropped Ben, then flew up in the sky and ran away in fear. Then I fell on the ground due to fatigue.

When I woke up, Ben was sitting down close to the lake, skipping rocks.

When he noticed that I was awake, he ran up to me and said in excited tone, "How did you do that?"

Suddenly, my dream shifted. I saw myself and Vincent hiding behind boxes in a throne room. Again, I saw a gold coffin in the middle of the room. I also saw Wyatt in a king's chair. He and some centaurs were talking about an invasion.

"Capture Max Iverson and Vincent Fletcher because I know they're in here somewhere. Now go!" Wyatt demanded.

In an instant, they ran quickly, but I knew they were serving Wyatt out of fear. "We have to get out of here," Vincent whispered.

He pulled out his hand and quietly said, "Hand me the potion."

"Uh . . . what potion? I replied confusingly.

"What do you mean 'what potion?'!" he yelled.

I covered his mouth swiftly, and then I got out my watch to make for us invisible cloak.

"I heard them!" one centaur screamed.

"So did I!" another one shouted.

Due to invisibility, they couldn't find us. Then I turned to Vincent, and I asked again, "What potion?"

"The potion to get us out of here," he said, trying to sound calm. "Okay, we can solve this out ourselves. Run for your lives!"

Then he ran, and the centaurs detected him.

The invisibility cloak stopped working as soon as he ran.

"Well! Well! Well! If it isn't Vincent, son of Apollo." He sneered at where I was hiding and said, "Where's your friend?"

"You'll never find him!"

"Him," he yelled. "Search the castle!"

Wyatt snapped his fingers, and then Vincent's quiver, bow, and arrows were equipped to him. "Excalibur," he said, and then a sword appeared in his hand.

The sword was about forty-five inches overall. It was maybe twenty-karat gold with a genuine leather handle and a dragon mark at the end of the handle. My eyes widened with fear, then that's when I remembered that it was the sword King Arthur removed from the stone.

"How did you summon Excalibur!" Vincent yelled.

"I went back in time, killed King Arthur, and brought out the sword from the stone." Vincent quickly grabbed an arrow and shot it straight at Wyatt's face. Smoke appeared around him, and then he started chocking. "Run!" Vincent yelled. "He's distracted now."

"I'm not leaving here without you," I replied. He smiled and ran down the hall, and I followed.

Yet again, my dream shifted. A girl was fighting a snake lady at a volcano. As soon as I looked closer, I noticed it was Grace who was fighting. Suddenly, the volcano erupted and earthquakes started. Hurricanes, tornadoes, every natural disaster was going on. Then I heard laughter. The laugh was sinister. The voice began to say something.

It said, "Max, you failed to save your world, and now mass chaos and destruction will occur." I was too frightened to continue the dream, and I made myself wake up. When I woke up, the people who served us snacks walked past me.

I knew it would be rude, but I just woke up from sleep, and I was grumpy, and so I confronted her. "Hey, you passed me!" I yelled.

Then her eyes began to look like a stray cat's. She hissed at me, and said, "Wait your turn."

No, she actually hissed at me. I knew she was a monster, so when she was walking back to the area where you get food, I followed her. When I got there, everything was calm.

Then one of the service managers bumped into me and said, "May I help you?"

"Um, no, thank you," I replied.

He then began to sniff me and said, "Half blood," in a baritone voice. I dug into my pocket to reach out for White Fang, but he stopped me. "No need to fight when we clearly have the upper hand," he told me.

"Who is we?" I asked demandingly.

"My fellow monsters on the plane," he said calmly.

I looked around and noticed that the service managers that served us food were all monsters. I ran back to my seat in terror.

"Vincent," I whispered, "did you know that this plane is infested with monsters."

"What!" he yelled.

But before he could further say something, I covered his mouth. "Shh!" I whispered.

"What do we do?" he said with a frightened look on his face.

"We play it cool, and we don't tell the others so they don't have to worry."

Suddenly, it felt as if the plane was landing. When I looked outside, I noticed the plane was falling.

"Vincent!" I yelled, but before I could tell him what to do, he said, "Already on it." And he headed toward where the pilot was. People on the plane started screaming and yelling. Clair, Jonah, and Cindy woke up.

"What's going on!" they yelled.

"The plane is crashing, and that's not the bad part," I replied.

"What is the bad part?" Jonah said.

"The plane is infested with monsters," I answered.

Their eyes widened, and they demanded, "Max, you have to use your powers to save us and stop the plain from crashing."

"How do I do that?" I said.

"Concentration!" I heard.

I closed my eyes and focused on my powers only. I focused on water, but nothing came to me. Then I had an idea. My eyes began to glow, then I knew, I knew that I could do something. I broke the earth in half and gathered any nearby water to the area we were in. Then as we crashed, we landed softly in the water. After we crashed, I made the water wash away. I fainted after that.

"Max, wake up," a voice whispered.

When I opened my eyes, it was Vincent trying to wake me up. When I got myself together, I noticed the service managers were fighting Clair.

"Max, we have to find a way out of here," Vincent whispered.

"What's going on?" I asked.

"No time to explain, just follow me," he said. Then a rumbling sound came from the ground.

"We have to hurry!" he yelled.

All of a sudden, a huge worm came out of the ground. It swung its tail, but swiftly, I got White Fang out of my pocket, uncapped it, and sliced the tail in half. For some reason, it regenerated. We kept running. "Kill any service manager you can find and split up."

I went north, and he went south.

"Whatttt a ssssurprisssssse," a service manager said to me.

I noticed it was the same monster I had encountered on the plane. I fixed myself in battle position, and I was ready to fight. This time, half of his body was all snake, and he had fangs instead of teeth. He slithered around me with intense speed and tried to bite me, but I dodged swiftly.

"Why are you all doing this!" I yelled.

He laughed sinisterly and said, "For the sssssake of our

masssssster Kronosssss."

I thought in my head that if this Kronos guy could gather these many monsters, he must be strong.

CHAPTER 6

STRANDED

I was out powered, so the only thing I could do now was run. I ran at full speed, thinking, Why am I doing this? No one asked me to be a half blood. No one said I had to do these dangerous missions. Then I thought to myself that more people needed my help and that's what I was going to do. I kept running, yet the snake monster kept following me.

"Max!" a voice yelled.

When I turned, it was Jonah trying to give me his electric spear to fight the monster instead of my sword. He threw the spear like a javelin, and luckily, I caught it. Static surged through the spear like a lightning rod. I grabbed hold of it more firmly, and then I stabbed the snake monster in the heart.

"Arhh!" he whined.

More electricity surged through the spear fiercely, and the monster blew up into orange smoke powder.

Before you knew it, all my friends had destroyed all the other monsters. Vincent ran toward me and asked me, "Are you okay?"

"Yeah, I'm fine," I said "and what about the others?"

"They are coming," he replied.

Once Jonah reached us, I tossed his spear to him, and it

transformed back to a regular knife. "What do we do about the mortals?" Jonah asked.

"We can cast a sleeping portion on them until we find the airport," Cindy suggested. Vincent nodded his head down and began to think for a second.

"That could work, but we don't have any on us now, plus the potion wouldn't be strong enough to put all of them to sleep," Clair said.

"Max, can you use your powers again to split the island in half from the humans and us?" Vincent asked me.

"I think I can," I replied. I closed my eyes and focused on drifting two parts of the island, but nothing happened.

"Maybe I can help," a crippled old voice said from a dark shadow.

"Reveal yourself!" Jonah yelled.

Then a man with the crippled old voice stepped out of the shadow. He was old with a torn-up black rag that he wore as a jacket with a hood on. He was probably two and a half feet tall.

When I looked at Vincent, he looked agitated. All of a sudden, he busted out and yelled, "You foolish, stupid old man, you can't help us because you're wrinkled up and shriveled!"

I pulled Vincent down and asked him, "What was that all about?"

"He thinks we're desperate, plus we don't need his help," Vincent continued.

"He has, maybe, lived on this island for decades," I replied. "He might know the way."

"If he knew the way, why would he still be on this stupid island?" Vincent yelled.

"Let's just see what he has to say," I said gently.

"I can lead you to where you need to go," the old man said. When he started to walk, we followed.

As we went farther into the island, I wondered what my dad looked like and whether he was nice and respectful.

"Are you all half bloods?" the old man asked.

We looked at each other, knowing that we couldn't tell

mortals our secret, and we stayed quiet. "Well?" the old man said in a mad, frustrated tone.

"Yes, we are half bloods," Jonah answered.

"Jonah!" all yelled except for me.

"Look, if he already knows about the Greek world and that the gods are still alive, then there is no reason in hiding the truth from him," Jonah said intelligently.

Vincent sighed in despair and told him, "Whatever."

When we continued to walk, Vincent asked, "Hey! Old man, how do you know about the Greek world?"

The old man turned and smiled faintly. We noticed that it was almost nighttime.

"Let's settle here," the old man suggested. The old man told Jonah to get firewood, and he did.

"By the way," I said, "what is your name?"

"Heh! Heh!" he chuckled. Then he began to say, "It is Noland, kid."

"Why are you helping us?" I asked.

"Because without my guidance, in a matter of thirty minutes, you all would die," he replied. We were stunned to hear what he had said.

"He's just kidding," Vincent bragged to lighten the mood.

Noland knew we wanted to know how we couldn't survive on this island, so he began to tell about the past of this island.

"It all started when the age of the Titans began. In the middle of the war, the gods and Titans were so fond of destroying each other. Their anger and hatred created this island. When the labyrinth was destroyed, all the bad creations of the gods and Titans—for example, the Minotaur—were trapped here forever."

"So when the war ended, no more monsters came here?" I asked.

"Foolish boy," he mumbled. "Once the war ended, monsters choose to come here because they thought it would be the safest place to hide from the gods."

In my head, I thought he was a monster, since only monsters live on this island. From my facial expression, Noland knew that

I wondered who he really was.

He turned his head down and said, "I'll tell you all how I got on this island.

"Long before you all were born, I went to Magic School, and my parentage was Zeus. All our faces were hard. As all of you may already know, demigods whose parents are Zeus, Poseidon, or Hades have a certain aura that attracts monsters twice as much as a regular demigod. Anyway, when I was thirteen, they finally gave me a quest. They told me I had to go to this island and retrieve a golden caduceus that symbolizes Hermes, god of roads. The part they didn't tell me was that the island was infested with monsters. And I had to learn that the hard way. Like I told you before, since my father is Zeus, I was like a monster magnet."

Then I interrupted, "So if you know the way, why didn't you get off the island when you had the chance?"

"Because when people like you get on this island, I don't want them to end up the way I did," he responded.

I know it would be rude to ask, but I asked anyway. "How old are you?"

"A millennia," he answered.

As soon as he said that, our mouths dropped open. "But that's—"

"Before you say anything," he interrupted, "the only reason I'm this old is because when you're on this island for a long time, you age three times as much."

"But how are you still alive?" Vincent asked.

"I was just about to get to that part," he muttered. "The island keeps you immortal if you live on it for a while. Kids, it's time to sleep."

"Um! Where do we sleep?" I asked.

He knew all our stuff was still on the plane.

"Heh heh! You kids know nothing of the farm life, do you?"

I wanted to say, "This isn't even a farm, you crack head, this is an island," but I thought it would be rude. Without an argument, we slept on the ground. Even though I wasn't fully asleep, I saw Noland watch, guarding us. If you really think about it, he wasn't a cranky old man. He was a caring man.

Then I heard a noise. It was kind of like a stampede. Then the noise became louder and louder, and before you knew it, a Minotaur charged at Noland. He had the body of a bodybuilder and the head of a bull.

I got up and yelled, "Noland!"

He steadily got up. Then the Minotaur saw me. I got out White Fang and uncapped it, and the ballpoint instantly transformed into a three-foot-long sword. The mindless monster ran at me endlessly. I tried to jab my sword in his stomach, but he pounced on and aimed for my back.

By an inch, he missed. I thought of doing a hit-and-roll maneuver, but I guessed, if I did, when I rolled, he would just kick me. I therefore ran on top of one of the mini boulders that were stationed by our camp. As fast as I could, I jumped off the boulder and kicked the Minotaur in the head. It didn't really seem to affect him. It just angered him. I was mad because, upon all the noise that was happening, it didn't wake up my friends. He grabbed my leg and swung me like a lasso. My head hit the boulder hard. Everything was fuzzy now, and all I could see was a big black blur hurling toward me. I got my vision and my senses back together, and then I saw the Minotaur charging toward me. The monster was an inch from hitting me, but some arrow stopped it. When I turned, I saw Vincent with a bow in his hand.

"Vincent, how did you—"

"I made it from stick and string," he told me.

When Vincent shot the arrow, my friends woke up immediately. We quickly went to Noland's aid. "Take Noland and find some shelter while I distract the Minotaur," Cindy said bravely.

They ran and looked for shelter.

I ran to Cindy and said, "I'll help you."

"I don't need your help," she said angrily.

The Minotaur got up and charged. I uncapped White Fang, and before I could slash, it just stood there.

I turned around to Cindy, and she smiled and said, "I told I didn't need your help."

Then I figured out what had happened. Cindy's sweet scent clogged up the monsters sense of smell.

This is because the Minotaur can only move by scent. "What are you waiting for? Attack it!" Cindy yelled.

I finally stabbed the monster in the stomach, and it blew up into a red liquid. When I turned to follow Cindy, she was already gone.

"Cindy!" I yelled. No answer.

I began to worry that maybe she was dead. I ran to every spot thinkable and still didn't find her or any of my friends for that matter. I didn't know what happened, but I was going to find out. I thought of what way I could find them, and I had an idea. The whole island was covered with sand, and as they walked, they left footprints, so I could track them down using footprints.

"Not so fast, fish boy," a voice said behind me. I turned and saw no one. Then something grabbed me, and then I passed out. When I woke up, I was in a wooden cabin on a comfortable soft bed the size of eighteen beds put together. It felt like I was in heaven. Then I realized that someone, something had put me here. I got up, and I had on red pajamas with woolly mammoth socks. I walked, and I felt a little bit weary, but I forced myself to move on.

"Please don't move," someone said in a sympathetic tone. I quickly reached in my pocket for White Fang, but it wasn't there.

I turned and saw myself facing a girl about my age. She had long brown hair, hazel eyes, and looked lonely.

"Please don't go," she said.

For some reason, I was oddly attracted to her. I walked toward her, and I was too nervous to speak. "What's your name?" she asked me.

"Ma-Ma-Max," I stuttered.

"Would you like some tea?" she said sympathetically again.

She walked to the counters and made hot water. I knew this was just an act, so I tried to run. Suddenly, I caught myself in a beautiful song. It was the most beautiful song I had ever heard. It was like one of those baby nursery songs. It was so sweet that it made me change my mind and stay. All of a sudden, a loud sound came from the side of the wall. Cindy and my friends had busted through the wall.

"Freeze! Siren!" Vincent yelled.

Then Jonah closed his eyes and meditated. After that, he began to levitate in the air, and I was shocked. I realized that the cabin started to catch on fire.

"Where did that come from?" I yelled.

"Jonah is doing it, idiot," Cindy said.

I felt awkward because usually Cindy was very kind to me. Again, the girl started to sing. I felt weak and useless, but my body moved anyway. I was under a trance, and I don't want to sound late or stupid or anything, but I thought the girl was singing to control me. White Fang appeared in my hand even though I seemed to have left it in my other pants. The sword was even brighter silver and shinier than usual. Also the tip was razor sharp. I moved quickly, though I didn't make myself do it. I slashed Vincent on his chest, and he had a deep cut. I took another swing, then Jonah came out of nowhere and blocked with his own sword. His sword looked exactly like mine lengthwise, but the color was solid gold. Then a piece of his sword chipped off. My new and improved sword was so good that it chipped a piece off Jonah's sword. I didn't even know that he had a sword. I had thought he used an electric spear. Anyway, I wanted to tell them that I wasn't doing this willingly, but I couldn't move my mouth.

"Vincent, make use of yourself and kill the siren!" Jonah yelled.

Jonah barely held his sword with one hand. Then he used his other hand to dig in his pocket and handed his knife to Vincent. Then it transformed into a spear.

"How do you work this thing?" Vincent asked stupidly.

"Vincent, stop playing around!" Jonah yelled again, irritated.

"Okay!" Vincent replied.

Then a pure blue lightning shot straight at the girl. She dodged with no problem. She began to sing more, then I threw my sword at Vincent. His arm was mortally bruised, and I felt bad.

"Ow!" he screamed.

The girl started laughing, and I was getting madder by the second. I forced myself to resist the song, but it didn't work. I kept charging and slashing, and my resistance had no effect. Cindy went to Vincent's aid, and Jonah kept struggling.

I remembered what I read in the myths on how to kill a siren. Pierce its heart with an ice-cold object or take its lungs and rip it out. And you already know which one I was going to do. Rip her lungs out. I know it may sound nasty or creepy, but I was just tired of hearing that song.

I just stood still and concentrated. I tapped into my inner self and broke free of the song. I turned quickly, and then ran toward the siren. I aggressively stuck my sword in her mouth all the way to her stomach. It was too nasty to get my sword, so I left it. After a while, she blew up into pure liquid. I took my sword, and I ran to Vincent to ask him whether he was okay.

"Max, go find anything you can around this cabin," Jonah said seriously.

I walked farther into the warm cabin that was nearly burned down. I found a card on the floor, and it said, *Ezinna's Village Estate* (God is Honor, Hope, Promise, Justice, Love) Location: Mountain of Peace, Nigeria, West Africa.

"Jonah!" I yelled. "I found something."

He ran faster than a cheetah, and he asked, "Where did you find that?"

"On the floor," I replied.

His face darkened, and he told me, "Let's try to find more items."

As we went even farther, there was a big room that looked like an office. It had a clean oak writing desk and an executive black leather office swivel chair. The room looked pretty neat, but the only thing that seemed awkward was that the rest of it was empty. There was only one other object in that big room, and it was the coin we saw.

As we walked toward it, it wasn't a coin. It was a drachma, a golden drachma to be exact.

Drachmas are those weird Greek coins that are like a fortune in Rome and Greece. "What do we do with it?" I asked

"You keep it until we have a reason for using it," Jonah advised. I put it in my pocket, and we went back to the living room.

"We are ready," Cindy said tiredly.

While my friends were regaining their strength, I found the room where my clothes were, and I changed. When I finished, I walked back to the living room. After I said what had happened, we left.

"Noland!" Vincent yelled.

He came behind the tree and said, "Let's go."

We didn't really walk a long distance, but we were all tired except for Noland.

He was overexcited and kept trying to whip us in shape by saying, "Let's go, slowpokes," and, "my dead grandma can walk faster than you all."

He was about to say another statement when Vincent screamed, "Shut up!" I nudged him hard and whispered, "That's really rude."

He sighed and stormed off.

I was behind everybody, and I moved slowly. "Almost there," Noland commented.

We finally reached the airport, and it was bigger than the last one. It was mainly glass on the outside with an inscription, "The International Airport, Lagos"

"Oh no!" Cindy said.

"What is it?" I asked.

"We left the mortals on the other part of the island," she replied. She ran to the entrance of the airport and waved her right hand.

We followed her quickly. When we reached her, we saw her talking to a man dressed in uniform. The uniform was light green and had a badge on the side of his arm that had these initials: NFO— meaning Nigerian Federal Officer. That's when we finally realized that we were in Lagos, Nigeria. The man pulled out a walkie-talkie, and then a whole bunch of other people dressed the same came running out of the entrance.

Cindy came back to us, and then we all yelled, "What did you say?"

"I told the man over there that people were stranded on the other side of the island."

"So where do we get our luggage?" I asked.

"Over there," Cindy pointed.

We saw a man take some bags that looked like our stuff, and it was our stuff. We ran to him and ordered him to give us our bags back. The man was about in his sixties, had a Hawaiian shirt and brown pants.

"Let go of me! Let go of me!" he shouted with an African accent.

Then the whole stuff in the bag fell out. All we saw were underwear and empty cologne bottles. "Du you see! Du you see! See what you have done now!" he shouted again in African accent. Then we laughed.

"What are you laughing at, stupid little children?"

"You!" we all said.

"I hope Ezinna catches you!" he yelled and walked off.

"Did he just say Ezinna?" I asked.

"Maybe he's got some answers on how to find him," Vincent protested. Then he ran after the man. We could hear the man shout, "What do you want from me! Get off me, you hooligan."

We ran toward the man and ripped Vincent off. "You know Ezinna?" I asked the man. "Everybody knows him, he's just a myth."

"What do you mean he's just a myth?"

"I've spoken too much now, leave me alone!" Then he walked off.

"What if the guy that Chiron told us to find isn't real?" I asked my friends.

"Trust me, he's real," Jonah said.

"Look, there go our bags!" Vincent shouted. We walked to the bag area and grabbed them.

"So where do we go now?" Cindy questioned.

"We go and find a taxi to drive us to Mountain of Peace, right," I told them.

"First, let's exchange our money and find a hotel to sleep at." Vincent yawned. Then we went out and tried to find some dealers.

CHAPTER 7

❁

WE MEET SOME FISHY DEALERS

Being here in Nigeria for the first time wasn't all that nice. There were cars and motorcycles going out of control without signs, lanes in uncoordinated patterns and proportion, and motorcycles would come like a swarm of locusts from all directions, halfway short of running us over. They dived, cornered, turned, scooped, sped, slowed, and stopped in uncontrollable manner and with no respect to other road users. We were in wonderment if it was all a reality because we had never faced or experienced this level of chaos.

When one of them almost hit us, I could hear Cindy scream, "What are you doing?"

But I must be frank; I do not know how they did not hit one another all the time. That's when I realized that these people must be smart to operate under that chaos with no casualties. We were any way still confused.

The worst part about it was people were staring at us as if we were some kind of freaks. Every time we asked one of them where Ezinna was, they looked at us as if we were crazy. We kept walking, looking for dealers who could exchange our U.S. dollars into Naira. The walk was long, and my backpack and my

67

luggage felt heavy. Most of the valuable stuff I had were just inside my backpack.

So I had an idea. There was a river about twenty miles away from me. Without telling my friends, I walked toward the river. As I kept walking, people looked at me in fright. When I reached where I wanted to go, I emptied my luggage and put everything in the backpack.

I know, why do all this?

Because it's stupid to carry different things at once when you can just put everything in just one bag.

When I finished, I threw everything that I emptied in the river.

When I turned back to find my friends, they were nowhere in sight. After a few minutes of searching for my friends, I bumped into someone. He was a man. He had a yellow African cap on, yellow shirt and pants and had a wad of cash in his hands.

"Um, can you exchange my money?" I asked.

His eyes widened, and he said, "Me no speak English. Me no speak English."

"Please, sir, I'm begging you," I told him desperately.

"Okay!" he replied.

He didn't really seem to have an accent when he spoke English. "So how much do you want to exchange?" he asked.

I dug in my pocket and tried to find the hundred-dollar bill I had. Then I found it. As soon as I pulled it out, he snatched it from me. He looked at it in delight. If this were a cartoon, his eyes would've probably lit up with the dollar sign.

He asked me how I wanted my money. "In fifties," I said.

He pulled out a big amount of money and just handed it to me without seeing how much he gave me.

When I turned to thank him, he was still looking at the hundred-dollar bill I gave him.

I then bumped into somebody again, but it was just Cindy. She yelled, "Where have you been?"

But that's just Cindy's way of saying, "Oh! Max, are you okay?"

I pulled the money I had gotten from the man, and she

suddenly got over the fact that she was mad at me. Behind were the rest of my friends. They were happy too.

"Should we go find a hotel now?" Vincent said tiredly.

"I know a hotel we can go to," Jonah blurted out. As he led us to the hotel, he told stories of him and his step dad always going there to hang out and how great the service and the food were.

"If it's so great, what's the name of it?" I asked.

"Rose Gate Hotel," he replied.

When we finally reached where he said the hotel was, we didn't really think it was the hotel that he said was the best. The words of the neon sign were nearly faded, and the building was dirty and had words on the side of the wall, saying, "It's the government's fault" and "Boo the government."

"Jonah, are you sure this is the hotel?" I asked him.

"Certainly," he replied.

We walked in, and we saw a guest clerk sleeping with a political magazine on his face.

"Hello," I said quietly.

When I said it, he jumped up and replied by saying, "Huh."

"May we please have a room," Cindy told him. He told us to come and to sign a release form, saying, "If any injuries may occur, we are not responsible and will not allow lawsuits."

He pointed where to sign, and I put some random guy's name. He added that since we signed, our stay here is free. Then we all said, "Thank you, sir," and we left a one-hundred-Naira tip, and he grinned as he picked it up, and then he smiled with his broad yellow teeth showing.

Cindy elbowed me and whispered, "Why are you putting other people's names?"

I told her, "So if one of us gets injured and we go to court and he shows them the contract, we can say that it is a false name." She hit me in my stomach and asked the clerk for the room number. He gave us the key and told us the room number was 601. We walked up the staircase and noticed the steps were an inch close from breaking. When we found our room, we all got mad at Jonah.

"It is not my fault the hotel isn't as good as it was last time," Jonah muttered.

I looked around the room a little, and I wasn't satisfied. The bed was dirty and filled with swarms of flies around it, the bathtub was like a mansion of roaches, and we had a view right next to a dumpster.

"Can't we demand a new room?" Clair asked.

"I'll do it," Vincent suggested.

"I'll go with him," Jonah also said. Cindy shook her head, and they ran off.

"So what do we do in the meantime?" I asked.

"We call Chiron and tell him our quest so far," Cindy replied.

I pulled out the mirror, which was in my pocket, and I knocked on it. When the mirror began to glow, Drake appeared. On the right side of his face was a big deep red scar.

"Drake, what happened!" I yelled.

"Oh, it's nothing," he replied while looking at the ground.

"Drake, tell me," I demanded.

"Well, a quest went sour," he told me. He also told me he would tell me when I get to Magic School.

"Oh, and where's Chiron?" I asked.

"He's not here right now," he said. "Try calling later." Then he signed off.

"So what did Chiron say?" Cindy asked.

"Drake answered," I told her.

"I'm going to go get something to eat," Clair said.

I quickly got mad and yelled to Clair, "You lazy, selfish, bigheaded, spoiled brat."

"Max!" Cindy screamed at me.

Clair turned to me and said, "What did you say?"

Before I could say what I wanted to say, Cindy told Clair that I was just playing with her. When she left, Cindy yelled, "What were you thinking!"

"She has done nothing this whole entire trip and she acts as if she was our savior."

"Max, do you know who she is?" she asked me.

"Yeah, I do. She is a bigheaded snob," I replied. "No, she is the daughter of Athena."

"If she's the daughter of a smart god, why is she as dumb as rubber," I joked.

"She has been planning battle strategies since we offered her to go on this trip with us," she commented.

"Then how come she never told us?"

"She didn't have to," Cindy said and walked off.

I went to the dinner area and saw Clair crying and Cindy trying to cheer her up. I overheard their conversation, and Clair said, "Max is right, I am a spoiled brat."

Cindy rubbed her hand on Clair's back and said, "That's not true." I walked off the corner I was in and said, "Sorry for what I said." Clair wiped her tears and told me it was okay.

"So where's the food?" I asked. I looked to the left and saw different food on the table. On top of that was a sign that said, "Serve Yourself."

We ran there, grabbed some plates, and took anything we wanted on the plate. I took mashed potatoes, sweet yams, Chinese rice, and chicken. When we sat back down, I was about to demolish my food when Cindy said, "Stop. Max, before demigods eat, we always offer a sacrifice to the gods."

"Oh!" I replied.

They raised their hands, and I followed.

Clair and Cindy chanted, "We sacrifice this meal to you." Then they threw some of their food to the fire next to us.

"To Athena!" Clair yelled. "To Aphrodite!" Cindy yelled.

"To Poseidon!" I yelled. "Now we can eat, right?"

"Yes!" Clair replied.

I stuck everything in my mouth all at the same time (exaggerating). When I realized that I forgot to drink anything, I barely stood up and walked back to the table where the food was. I picked up a two- liter bottle of Mountain Dew and drank the entire thing. Cindy and Clair laughed at me, and I felt happy.

"Now!" Cindy yelled.

"Let's not fight our parents' battles and start a good friendship,"

Cindy declared. "Which parents' battles do you mean?" Clair asked.

"Stupid, did you not know about the rivalry and feud between . . ."

After that, Clair and I shook hands, and we all hugged and then declared, "No parents' battles shall stand between us, friends for now, friends forever."

"Now let's find Jonah and Vincent," I announced.

We left the room after that. When we entered the lobby, no one was there. Then there was a power outage.

"Ahh!" Clair screamed.

"Calm down, Clair," Cindy demanded.

"Can't you use your intelligence to make light with your bare hands?" I asked. Cindy elbowed me and told me to stop making jokes.

Clair said she would try.

"Clair, it was just a joke," Cindy told her.

"No, my mother is watching over me and seeing what decisions I make, and I'm going to give her a reason to love me," Clair told us.

She put out her hands, and she touched her way through. I think she found some items and fused them together since I heard a lot of noise.

"Ahh!" a voice screamed.

"Clair!" Cindy yelled.

We ran back to the dining room and saw a giant glowing snake. It was strangling Clair. "Clair!" I yelled.

Drops of blood trickled down her cheek. The snake opened its mouth and spat at us. We both dodged. When we looked back, the wall was melting where the snake had spat.

"Nitrogen acid," Cindy muttered.

"What do you want with Clair?" I demanded.

"I want to make her my hostage," the snake said.

"Max," Cindy called, "it's not a monster, it's a mutated snake."

My eyes opened widely. "What?" I replied.

"The traitor must've put the harmless snake in nitrogen acid and sent him to Nigeria and also charmed him to find us and kill us."

"Who sent you?" I asked.

"I was charmed not to say his identity," the snake replied.

Then the snake strangled Clair some more. After that, I ran fast toward the snake. I quickly uncapped White Fang, and it lit the whole room up. I charged at the snake, and he dodged by slithering. Then he spat at me again, and I used my sword as a shield. It didn't melt. It just rusted. All of a sudden, Clair lifted herself up backward and kicked the snake in the face. Then she broke loose of the snake's choke hold.

"Clair, how did you do that?" I asked in amazement.

"I had one thousand more battle strategies on how to escape," she said, being modest.

The snake slithered toward us faster than he would usually. When he reached us, he tried to bite Cindy at the neck, but Clair karate-kicked him away. When I tried to stab the snake with the sword, the sword didn't affect him at all.

"The sword can only affect supernatural beings!" Cindy yelled at me. Then the snake knocked the sword out of my hand.

"Stupid snake!" I yelled.

"The name is Barbus," he commented.

"Stupid Barbus!" I corrected.

Cindy got out her pocketknife and stabbed Barbus. Blue liquid oozed out where Cindy had stabbed him.

"Ahh!" Barbus screamed. "I surrender," he whined.

"Tell us who sent you," I demanded.

"I was charmed not to say," he said.

"Well, can't you just break that charm?" I replied.

Cindy chuckled and said, "When you are charmed, it's like putting a zipper on your mouth."

"Exactly," Barbus commented. "End my living existence, and I'll tell you."

Cindy stabbed him, and his body caught on fire.

"As long as I'm still alive, I can't tell you." Barbus said.

"What!" I yelled.

"But I will give you one clue. It's someone you trust the most," Barbus whispered. Then he blew up. Then the power turned back on.

"Let's go find Jonah and Vincent," I said.

After we discussed where we should go, we went to the lobby. The man still wasn't there.

"Vincent!" I yelled.

"Jonah!" Cindy yelled.

My mind really wasn't focused on finding my other friends. I was focused on what Barbus had said. It's someone you trust the most, I thought in my head. Maybe it could be Cindy, but she was there since she was six, and she's too bright to be a traitor.

What if Clair was the traitor? But she doesn't really act as if she wants to bring Kronos back, I said in my head. There were a whole lot of suggestions. But I have to focus on my mission, I thought in my head again.

"Let's go back to the room, and maybe they'll come to us," I suggested.

"We can't just leave them," Clair said.

Then I remembered my telepathy link with Jonah. I closed my eyes and concentrated and removed my head from any disturbing thoughts. Then my mind began to relax, and for a moment, I felt peace until I heard Cindy saying that Jonah and Vincent were back.

But I couldn't stop the telepathy link, and I started to get massive headaches. I fell to the ground holding my head due to my headache. I started to be stressed, and I felt blood seeping out my mouth. After a while of headaches, they finally stopped, and I passed out. I woke up in our hotel room, and I could hear Jonah arguing with Cindy about why she didn't stop me from using the link. When I had enough strength, I muttered, "It wasn't her fault."

"Max!" everybody yelled.

They came to me and helped me stand up.

When I was face-to-face with Jonah, I said to him, "It wasn't Cindy's fault. It was mine, and I knew the dangers of the telepathy link."

He grabbed me by the shirt and said, "You don't know the half of it. When you are two feet away or less, the person using the telepathy link will be on the verge of dying," he continued.

"I'm sorry," I replied.

He kept quiet, and then he asked, "Have you contacted Chiron?"

"Yeah, I have, but Drake answered."

"Jonah, a mutated snake named Barbus attacked us," Clair said.

"What!" he replied? "Did you all get hurt?"

"No, but he said something about the traitor," I replied.

"Well, did he say who it was?" he asked.

"No, but he gave us a clue. 'It's someone you trust the most.'"

Jonah nodded his head down and said, "Let's stay a few nights and see what we'll do from there."

"Um, what about some privacy," the girls said.

"They're right," I said.

"Since there is nobody, we can get any room we want," Vincent said happily.

"I will call top floor!" Cindy yelled.

"So do I!" Clair yelled as well. Then they both ran and so did we.

We ran and found the stairs to the upper floor. When we reached there, it looked like a paradise. There were mini pools, indoor soccer stadium (which was awkward), cotton candy machines, game systems, and wide screen TVs and more machines that had to do with candy and treats. I ran and jumped in one of the pools, and the water splashed everywhere. Vincent ran to the cotton candy machine, made some cotton candy and dipped his head into the machine. The girls went to the game systems, which was really a guy's thing. Jonah sprinted to the pool and jumped into it.

After a while of relaxing in the hot water, Jonah asked me, "Do you want to play soccer?"

"Sure," I replied. When I got out, I was completely wet. I thought of being dry, and then I was. I was too excited to really care how I did it.

"Max, dig fast!" Jonah yelled.

When I turned, I saw a soccer ball heading toward me like a torpedo. I jumped out the way of getting hit. I ran after the ball and kicked it back. He came toward me, doing tricks with the ball. I dove in with my foot and stole the ball.

"How about we do some sword practicing," I suggested.

"Sure," he replied.

He brought out his own sword. I uncapped White Fang, and I prepared to fight Jonah. I swung first, but he dodged by gliding backward. He dug his sword into the ground then ran sideways. I swiftly ran to his sword, then I tried to grab it, but he quickly jumped on his sword. He started to conduct energy and electricity. Suddenly, his sword burned with fire. I noticed my friends witnessing what was happening. Jonah's body was then surrounded with currents of electricity. Then I figured out what he was going to do. He jumped off his sword and hit me with full force. It hurt more than it was supposed to because the punch was filled with electricity. I fell on the ground, sobbing due to the fact that my stomach was hurting nonstop. Jonah removed his sword from the ground and looked at me with a smile. He walked toward me and helped me up. When I gained balance, I kicked his calf, and he fell. He back flipped and started to catch his breath. I made sure he wasn't close enough to me so I could use the telepathy link.

I know. Why would I use it again after what happened before? I was willing to take chances. I closed my eyes and concentrated. I was now reading Jonah's mind. For some reason, he wasn't aware of it. I wanted to read his mind, to find out how he did that move without concentrating. The only answer was meditating. Now I understood why he always meditated when he had free time. When I tried to read more of his thoughts, he blocked me out. I opened my eyes, and I saw him smiling. When I was just about to make a mini earthquake, an arrow smoked the soccer field, and neither of us could see.

"I can't just sit here and watch you hog all the fun," a voice said.

When the smoke disappeared, I saw Vincent in the middle of the soccer field, standing where Jonah and I were fighting. His quiver was at his back, and his bow was in his hand. Vincent shot another arrow, but he shot it in the air. A few seconds later, a rain of other arrows lashed down where Jonah and I were.

"Take this!" Vincent yelled.

He shot another arrow, but this time, the arrow was in the form of a glove. Bam! It hit Jonah instantly on his face.

"Your turn," Vincent said to me.

He grabbed another arrow out of his quiver. I then began to make a mini earthquake that could take out the whole of Lagos. Suddenly, there was a rumble from the ground. Then Vincent started to try and get balance, but it was useless. He fell to the ground. It seemed only the soccer field had the affect of the earthquake. He managed to put the arrow in the bow. I instantly grabbed White Fang and uncapped it. Then it sprung into a sword form. I ran as fast as I could to Vincent and cut his bow in half.

"No!" Vincent yelled. "I have had it!"

"Oh no!" Cindy said.

"Cover your ears!" Clair yelled.

"Aaaaaaaaa!" Vincent screeched ultrasonic sound waves. They were so powerful it made me fly all the way to a wall. I fell down and passed out. I woke wondering where I was. Everything was still a blur.

"You really got to stop passing out like that," Cindy said to me. "Here, drink this." The drink was yellow and smelled like vanilla. I immediately drank it.

"Urrh!" I grunted. Suddenly, my pains eased off. I got up and asked, "Where's Jonah and Vincent?"

"They're trying to prepare our departure," Clair answered.

"We are leaving already?"

They didn't answer. They both got up and said, "Let's go." I followed them downstairs all the way to our room.

"Everybody set?" Jonah asked.

"Yeah," we replied.

"Um! Sorry about before," Vincent said. "No problem," I replied.

When we walked out of the hotel, we tried to figure out how we were going to go to Mountain of Peace. I was surprised because it was nighttime.

"Are you serious?" I complained.

"Mountain of Peace is all the way in the east. Once we get to the east, we will find Mountain of Peace and walk to Ezinna's Palace Village Estate."

"So what do we use to get to the east anyway?" Cindy said.

"How about we buy some new clothes and book bags. I remembered a nearby clothing store.

Follow me," I said as I ran off.

When I finally found it, they were closed. "So what do we do now?" I asked.

"We break in," Vincent said.

It was quite awkward because children of Hermes had a habit of stealing things, but he was a child of Apollo. Anyway, we still broke in. Everybody got what suited them, changed, and left.

I wore a red shirt, a new pair of jeans, a black jacket without a hood, and a pair of white Nikes with a dark blue backpack.

"Instead of paying a lot of money taking private or public transportation, we can go to a magical train station," Cindy suggested.

"Let's do this then," I said.

Vincent pulled out a potion from his pocket and threw it in the air. We all jumped in as a portal appeared. In no time, we were already there at the station. We saw a female gargoyle standing at the lever that lets the train go.

"Where to?" the gargoyle asked.

"The east," I replied.

"That would be eight golden drachmas, please," she demanded.

I dug in my pocket and found that one golden drachma that we found in the cabin at the island.

"Um! Ma'am, may you please accept this one golden drachma

because it's all that we have," Vincent said, trying to pretend a sobbing.

"If it is all that you have, how come your clothes look so new?" the gargoyle replied in a gentle way.

Vincent ran to the lever and pushed the gargoyle on the ground far away from the lever. "Make a run for it!" Vincent shouted as he pulled the lever.

As the doors to the train opened, we all ran into the train. "What about you?" I asked Vincent.

"I'm gonna get on the train. Just get in," he replied.

Once we got in, he jumped and barely made it into the train. When the gargoyle noticed that the train was about to leave to take off, she sprouted her wings, flew to the lever, and tried to stop the train from continuing, but it was too late. I could see the gargoyle jumping up and down, throwing a tantrum.

CHAPTER 8

DISASTER TO THE EAST

Cindy walked up to Vincent, slapped him on the head, and yelled, "Why did you do that? Because of that little stunt you pulled, we won't be able to use magical transportation again."

Jonah and I walked back toward Vincent and pulled him back. Then we started laughing. "Nice job," Jonah told Vincent.

"Yeah, man, you're the best," I said again. "When did you get the nerve to do that?" I said. He kept quiet and laughed.

"So how long is the trip?" I asked Jonah. "Look up," he said. I looked up at a metal bar with a sign that said,

Departure: 9:50 pm

Arrival: 6:25 am

I asked the team, "How about we just sit down and chillax?"

Clair and Cindy went on the left side of the chairs. Jonah, Vincent, and I went on the right side of the chairs. Clair brought out her iPod, then Cindy and Clair started listening to it.

"So what do we do?" I asked Jonah and Vincent.

All of a sudden the train lights went off, and the train began to stop. The doors opened. After a while, they shut back. Then the lights came back on. We saw a boy about our age standing close to the entrance doors.

I quickly uncapped White Fang and asked, "Who are you?"

The boy was wearing a brown shirt with a skull design on it and black pants. He had hazel hair.

"I'm not gonna ask again. Who are you?" I demanded.

"My name is Jake," he finally replied.

"Monster?" I asked.

"Half blood," he said.

"Who's your godly parent?" Jonah questioned. He chuckled and said, "Poseidon."

"What!" I yelled. "You can't be the son of Poseidon because I'm the only child of Poseidon."

"You're pathetic," he exclaimed and continued. "You are so short of knowledge that you don't even know that the gods are very fast. We are not even the first children of Poseidon. He has many more unclaimed half bloods just as strong as you."

I charged at him with White Fang because I couldn't stand the lies he was saying.

He quickly swung out his own sword and maneuvered through all my blows. Even though I didn't want to admit it, he was a good swordsman. He could even be better than Drake. He spun his sword when I attacked, and my sword flew out of my hand. I was open for an attack, but instead, he put his sword back in its sheet that was attached to his back and opened his hand out for a handshake. I then shook his hand.

When we sat down, I asked him, "Are you really a son of Poseidon?"

"Unfortunately, I am."

"Why 'unfortunately'?" I questioned.

"He didn't want to claim me, and he left my poor mother alone as soon as she had me. Then once he left, we didn't have enough money to pay the bills. At age four, my mother died and I was assigned to go to a foster home in New York. Then a year later, the foster home shut down, and I didn't have a place to stay."

"You never went to Magic School?" I asked.

"They never came due to the fact that I didn't show a sign of being a half blood. On my next birthday, Poseidon's messenger water spirit came and gave me a potion and two golden with a note on it. I read the note and did as it said. Before you know it, I was traveling to different places using the magical train. You could say I lived on the train."

"So you still live on the trains?"

"Yeah. Hopefully, I will find a family."

"So where are you going now?"

"To the Council of Enchanted Elders," he said.

"What!" Cindy outbursted. "You are going to ask them of your fate?"

"Yes," he replied.

"But half bloods that went to the Council of Enchanted Elders never made it back, and it is only meant for gods to go," Jonah exclaimed.

"Wait! Wait! Wait!" I said, trying to know what was going on. "First, what is the Council of Enchanted Elders?"

"A group of old men of different species that are to tell you of your fate," Cindy said.

"But back in the days, it was originally meant for the gods to do, until a very disobedient and bad half blood, son of Zeus, was told by his father to never go to the Council of Enchanted Elders that was stationed over the hilltop. Instead, the little boy insisted to go to the Council of Enchanted Elders, and so he did. He proudly demanded the council to tell him his fate. Once they did, the knowledge that the boy knew was too much for him to handle. Then the poor boy died of an information overload. From that point on, half bloods that went to ask their fate died before they could process the information in their heads."

"I know the story," Jake mumbled. "So where are you all going?"

"We are going to the east to see an old man named Ezinna."

"Oh!" He replied.

"It looks like your team and you aren't really trained," he announced.

"How dare you!" Jonah yelled.

Jake stood up and said, "If you think you're so tough, how about you battle me." Jonah pulled out his knife, and it turned into an electric spear.

Jake pulled out his sword.

If you really thought about it, the train space was pretty large in a way. Jonah shot fire out of his spear that was really unexpected because he said it only shot out electricity.

Then I asked Cindy, "Why did his spear shoot out of fire?"

"It can shoot out of fire too," she replied.

Jake used his sword to absorb the fire then waited for Jonah to strike again. Jonah jumped up and used his spear to strike Jake with electricity surrounding the spear. He struck fearfully, but Jake just countered it with his sword and used his elbow to knock out the spear out of Jonah's hand. The move he just pulled on Jonah was almost exactly similar to the move he used on me. Jake had an open shot, and he struck. Jonah fell down sobbing. Jake then grabbed Jonah's spear, but before he could hit Jonah with the spear, it shocked him.

Jonah smiled and said, "I'm the only one that chooses who possesses the spear." Then Jonah ran to the spear and attacked Jake. The pointy part of the spear pierced itself into Jake's stomach, and then he passed out. We waited until Jake woke up. A few minutes later, Jake woke up, but the electricity paralyzed him.

Clair walked up to me and said, "Do you notice there's something weird about Jake."

"Not really, except for the over competitive thing with him," I replied.

"I've informed all the others about it, and they said it was weird," I told Clair.

"Anyway, I'm going to ask him some questions," Clair said.

When we finished the conversation, she walked over to Jake and slapped him. Then she asked him fiercely, "Who are you really? And why are you going to the Council of Enchanted Elders."

"I'm never going to tell you!" he yelled back.

She slapped him again but even harder this time. "You're going there to learn Kronos's fate because he ordered you to go, didn't he!" She yelled. "And he also ordered you to meet up with us to befriend us and gain our trust, so at the last moment, when we have our backs turned, you'll try to kill us. And you would know our location because the traitor told you."

"All correct," he said while he laughed.

He then got up and got a potion out of his pocket and threw it on the ground, then he was gone. "Whoever knew Jake was a traitor?" Vincent said.

"But more importantly, how did you know, Clair?" Vincent asked.

"From the beginning, when he fought Max, I knew his fighting style was a little bit different and more agile, and half bloods fight in a more gentle way," she replied.

"So now, we contact Chiron, right?" Cindy suggested.

"Yeah," Clair replied.

Cindy dug in her backpack and brought the mirror out. Then she knocked on it. The mirror began to make the person's appearance, and then Drake answered.

"So how is your journey?" he asked.

"I don't have time," Cindy demanded. "I need to speak to Chiron immediately."

"Sorry, but Chiron is on a mission, but you can call later," he said exactly like he did last time. "Since when does Chiron go on missions," she replied?

"It was very urgent, and you have to understand," he said.

"Well, we'll call when we're coming back," she said. Drake then signed off.

"How about we sleep for now?" I said.

"You lazy bum!" Clair yelled. "All you think about is sleep."

"I'm the only one doing all the work!" I yelled back.

Suddenly, the train started to stop. Then we heard a buzzing sound at the entrance. Bam! The door busted open. When the dust from the door cleared up, we saw the monster. It was Ron.

"Ron!" Cindy yelled in surprise.

"But we saw him blow up into ash," Jonah remarked as well.

Something was different about Ron's face. The right side of his face looked scorched. And on the left side of his head, half of his hair was gone.

"Hah! Hah!" He laughed. "Kronos has brought me back to get my revenge on you," Ron said in a baritone voice.

"Did he also make you uglier?" Vincent joked. And everybody laughed. And his suit was half- scorched with patches of cloths gone.

"Arhh!" Ron threw a fireball at Vincent, but he missed.

"Ha! Ha! You missed," Vincent said, laughing.

"Shut up!" Ron yelled.

Suddenly, he was close to Vincent.

"He's gained super speed!" I informed everybody. Before Vincent could run, Ron caught him.

"Now you are going to suffer the fate I suffered when you killed me!" Ron screamed. I grabbed my sword and aimed for Ron's leg.

"Ah!" He yelled in surprise.

He dropped Vincent, and I charged at his other leg. "We need to blow this place up!" Vincent yelled.

I stopped stabbing Ron and jumped out the train and everybody followed. Luckily, there was a nearby magic mall that we could go to.

As Vincent jumped out, he shot an arrow, and the train blew up with Ron in it. Parts of the train that was left were on fire. A figure came out of the part that was on fire, which seemed to be the entrance. When the figure came closer to us, we saw Ron again. He was holding his right arm while his whole body was drenched in fire.

"I will not die until I get my revenge!" He yelled.

"Run!" Vincent yelled as he ran.

We ran to the inside of the mall. I was intimidated by the size of the mall. It could be bigger than the Empire State Building fused with two football fields.

When we were inside, Jonah said, "We should split up."

Vincent went with the girls while Jonah and I went together.

Jonah and I hid behind a clothes rack.

Ron sniffed and walked toward our direction.

Then he was behind me, and he whispered, "I could smell your fear." He touched Jonah, and then Jonah's flesh peeled off by fire . . .

"Jonah!" I screamed. I took my sword out and looked brave. I slashed Ron in the face along with some of the clothes on the rack.

I heard a sizzling sound coming from his cut. I dropped my sword and channeled my powers. Suddenly, I could sense water bursting from the pipes and the toilet. Then I could feel the power in my control. I formatted my hands toward Ron, and two tsunamis rushed to Ron. I could hear Ron's scream. When the water cleared up, there was no sign for Ron. All I saw was soaked clothes and Jonah coughing out water. "Jonah!" I yelled in excitement.

"What happened?" he questioned.

"I used my power and killed Ron again," I replied.

"That's good, so now we inform the others that we should look for another train station," Jonah said.

"Can we just hang out a little in the mall?"

"Sure, but only for a few hours," he said.

"First stop is to the game area," I said happily.

I ran and took out a map from a container that was close to the clothes rack and the entrance. I opened it up, saw all the areas that were in the mall. The bad thing I found out about the mall was that it only sold magical items like potions, swords, shields, communication mirrors, and more.

Jonah walked ahead of me and said, "Come on."

The first store that we went to was a store called Blackthorn Sword Shop. When we went in, the place was magnificent. The walls were shiny purple, different types of swords, sword sharpeners (small knifes that make your sword razor sharp), and beginner swordsman pamphlets that gave you tutorial lessons on how to use a sword. The other bad thing about the store was that it was very expensive.

The shop clerk was a human-sized red dragon. Smoke rose out of his nostrils, and he asked, "What are you here for?"

"Nothing, sir, we are just looking around," Jonah replied. "Are you going to buy something or not!"

"Sir," I said, "we are just looking around!"

"Security!" he shouted.

Then two big giants, not as tall to break the roof, chased us out of the store. As we were running, I asked, "What just happened?"

"The clerk told security to chase us unless we buy something," Jonah explained.

"Why?" I asked.

"Because in the Greek world, people want money fast, and if we don't give it to them and we are in their store, they'll even kill us," Jonah explained further.

"Let's hide over here," Jonah said.

We hid behind a corner and saw what the giants were doing. They were drawing pictures of us on sheets of paper and putting WANTED whoever turns them in will receive 80 drachmas.

We ran to where our friends were.

Cindy looked at us in shame. And she said, "I leave you knuckleheads alone for five minutes, and you are already wanted."

"I'm sorry, but we are getting that prize money," Vincent said happily.

"Don't mind Vincent," Cindy said. But we have to leave as soon as possible without the two of you being seen."

Then I suggested, "How about we trick the giants that you are turning us in, and when they give you the money, we run?"

"Agreed," everybody said.

Vincent and Clair held us at our wrists as if we had handcuffs. Before ten minutes passed, we were already in front of the giants. Also, a lot of creatures gathered in a circle around us, awing, sighing, and sobbing.

"You've captured the two," one giant said.

"Yes, and we want our prize money," Vincent demanded.

"Don't you think it's going to be a little bit hard escaping with all these creatures blocking all the exits?" I whispered to Jonah.

"We'll think of something," he replied calmly.

Both giants reached under the table behind them, which held more wanted posters. Then they both held up one bag of drachmas. It seemed there were forty in each bag.

As soon as they handed over the bags, Cindy yelled, "Run!"

Vincent and Clair took the money out from the giant's humongous hands and ran. Once we were free from them holding us, Jonah and I ran out of the store. As I ran, I could hear everybody yelling as well as the footsteps of the giants as they ran after us. Everybody followed Clair to the nearest train station. Once she did, the giants were getting closer and closer, and it took a long time to get to the train station. I had to think quickly, so I used my power to mess with the water pipes, and it sprayed them in the face, slowing them down in the process. Everybody jumped in the train, and the male gargoyle pulled the lever, and we were off.

I looked at the time board, and we had five hours left on this train. I was happy that we were almost there. Getting to Mountain of Peace was inevitable, but we still had to watch our backs. I thought of sleeping, but I knew if I did, bad things would happen.

"How do you think Magic School is holding up?" I asked Cindy.

"Not so good," she replied. "If the spy is still there, he might inform other operatives to delay our mission. And if that spy was able to know how to shut down the magical boundaries, he's been at Magic School for quite some time. So I think the spy is not someone that we know, because he wouldn't work for Kronos that is not older than thirteen."

"Say, if I were the traitor, would you expect it to be me?" I asked Cindy.

"No," she replied, "because, first, you don't have enough experience. Second, you haven't been in Magic School long enough to know how to shut down the magical boundaries. Third, you don't know many demigods, and last but certainly not the least, you are not strong enough."

"If you don't think I'm worthy enough to help, I'll just leave!"

"Good!" she yelled back.

I grabbed my book bag and looked at the time. Four hours and thirty minutes left. I decided to get out of the train and make it by myself. I pulled the bell so I could get off.

"No!" Vincent yelled.

"I'm sorry," I said and left, running. After a while, I was tired and started walking. "Come to your destiny," a voice said in a whisper with a baritone voice.

I suddenly looked back and saw no one. "Do not be afraid," the voice said.

But this time his voice was clear and deep.

"What do you want?" I yelled.

"Your trust," he replied.

"What's your name?" I demanded.

"You'll soon find out, but for now, keep walking forward," he said. My conscience told me not to, but my mind said I should, and I did.

As I walked, it became darker and colder. Then from a distance, I saw two old closed doors. The doors had black dragons, tornadoes, fires, and skulls.

"Good job," the voice said.

"You lead me to a trap!" I yelled.

"No, I didn't," he replied. "Open the doors."

I had a bad feeling about what was going to happen, but now my friends would never gonna wish I left. I pushed the doors open, and all I saw was a golden throne with thirteen high chairs. The tallest chair was in the middle and six chairs on both sides. There were only three people in the chairs.

"Welcome, Max Iverson," the person in the middle chair said. He had long gray hair and a zippered robe, which was black with a hood. As a matter of a fact, all three of them were wearing the same robe.

"What is this place?" I asked.

"Before you ask any questions, come in the middle of the throne," the voice said. When I walked, the doors closed. When I was in the middle, I looked up.

"Before I say anything, my name is Zemnas, and you've been chosen to join our organization."

"Which is?" I asked.

"The Black Hand," he said. "We consist of powerful demigods that pursue power."

"Why choose me? I'm just a kid." I asked.

"Even though you're a kid, you have the power and potential to be part of our organization."

"How did you find me?" I asked.

"We've been tracking you down since you were born, knowing destiny would bring us together."

"What do you want from me?" I asked.

"We want you to help us on our pursuit for power."

"And how do I do that?"

"First, you must wear our robe," Zemnas said.

"Are you kidding me?" the man on the right said aggressively.

"What is it, Xemas?" Zemnas asked.

"You're seriously going to add a kid to our organization?" Xemas asked. Xemas had long blue hair, two scars crossing each other, making an X. "Give the kid a break," the guy on the left of Zemnas said.

"Max, let me introduce you to two of the strongest members in our organization," Zemnas said. "On my left is Blaze."

Blaze had long red hair that stood up diagonally and had sharp green eyes. "On my right is Xemas."

"So what do I do now?" I asked.

Blaze stuck out his hand, and their robe was on me.

It fits perfectly, I said to myself. "So what is my mission? I asked firmly.

"Go to Mountain of Peace with Blaze and find a cavern not far from Ezinna's palace, then remove and enter it, and you will see a single giant crystal, and keep attacking it until it starts to glow. Then we'll have the power stored inside."

"What if I meet my friends there?" I asked.

"Terminate them," Zemnas replied.

Blaze teleported to me and waved his hand, and a vortex

appeared.

"Oh, and take this," Zemnas said.

Suddenly, the object appeared in my hand. It was a black ballpoint.

"Let me guess, it turns into a sword," I said boringly.

"You say it as if it were an ordinary sword. That is Pandora's Blade. Used for ultimate power, and it is invincible," he replied. "You'll know how strong it is when you use it."

Blaze and I went in the vortex, and in a split second, we were at Mountain of Peace.

CHAPTER 9

❋

WE WALK MOUNTAIN OF PEACE

It was the most beautiful place I'd ever seen. At Mountain of Peace, there were rainbows at every corner. Pegasuses were flying everywhere, birds chirping, and it was very peaceful. Green grass, green vegetables, spicy leaves, and shrubs are scattered about with flowers of yellow, blue, purple, and red petals. The smell of pollen was all over, and trees had fruits hanging to where you could just jump and pluck them to eat. Orange, mangos, bananas, grapes, pears, apples, peaches, guava, and paw-paw were abound.

Another thing spectacular about Mountain of Peace was the topography of the place. It was located on a plateau. There were undulating rolling hills, lakes, winding rivers, and a wild mix of savannah and scanty green forest vegetations, habitat of all kinds of animals in the universe. Reindeers, zebras, elephants, lions, deer, horses, the oldest tortoises, snakes, and pythons were all there. They moved around freely without any acting as predator.

And their humans, they looked as if they were sculptured in bright ebony—so peaceful and innocent as if they had just been born due to the smoothness and the refreshed look of their skins. They seemed to be in perfect harmony with their nature. There were no guns, spears, or arrows among these people that moved around. And most profoundly, they were extraordinarily polite and soft-spoken. In their kind and caring disposition, they acted and treated everybody like royalty.

As I was absorbed with this beauty of my lifetime, I forgot that Blaze was with me. I tried to get his attention, but from his fixated gaze he was also startled. We were really taken by what we saw.

As soon as Blaze turned to me, I asked, "So, Blaze, how do you know where the cavern is?"

"I know where it is because the organization told me," he replied. "Also, we've wanted to do this mission a long time ago, but we decided to let you do it instead. Instead of sitting, let's get to training before we head off to the cavern."

"What does the organization really want from me?" I asked.

"Nothing much, it's just that you have the power, intelligence, potential, and heart to join our organization. Ooh! And the whole thing that we've been tracking you down stuff and destiny bringing you here is all lies."

I huffed in a sign of relief. I brought out Pandora's Blade and uncapped it. Then I saw and felt the power of it. The blade was four feet long with black leather grip, and the blade part was super sharp and silver.

"Now that we've got that part done, charge me with everything you got," Blaze said.

"What?" I replied.

"You heard me. Charge at me," he repeated again.

Then I ran at full speed and attacked viciously. Suddenly he teleported medium-sized shrukens in each of his hands. The shrukens were decorated with fire. As soon as I was close enough, he counter attacked and struck with an open blow. I fell face-first. I slowly got up and panted.

"C'mon, you can do better than that," Blaze said, trying to annoy me.

Then I heard rumbling in the ground. Suddenly, something rose from the ground. Parts of its body were magma, the other parts were ground. It was huge.

"What is that?" I yelled.

"Real training practice," he replied.

Then I was confident. I jumped and attacked it repeatedly. When it swung, I dodged swiftly. The next time it swung, it hit me, hard. I fell down, sobbing. Then I quickly got up with a stern look. Suddenly, there was a sharp pain in my arm. I held my arm while Blaze was attacking it.

"This way!" a familiar voice yelled.

When the person with the voice started running, I saw Jonah. Then the rest of my friends came. "Max?" Cindy said surprisingly.

"Wow! Look up there," Vincent said.

Vincent pulled out his bow and arrows, then he shot at the monster. Jonah took out his spear and attacked as well. While Vincent and Jonah were attacking the monster, Cindy and Clair walked closer.

"Max," Cindy asked, "Why are you dressed in that robe?" I turned to the side.

"None of your business!" I yelled.

They flinched in shock. When I turned to the monster, it was crushing Blaze, making it impossible for him to breathe. Rage suddenly filled me. I stuck out my hand, and the earth started to come to life. The monster dropped Blaze, and the ground slowly turned it into a statue. Once it was fully a statue, I made a sword out of water in the other hand and extended the water sword to slice the monster in half. Then it blew up in shadow.

"Whow!" everybody except Blaze said. I felt as if it was no problem for me. Suddenly, I tapped into my inner self. All I could feel was darkness. When I woke from my inner self, I flipped my hood up. I grabbed White Fang, held it in my right hand and held the Pandora's Blade in the other.

"Prepare for an epic fight," I warned my friends. Blaze teleported out.

"Max, we are sorry," Cindy said.

"Come back! Heh," I replied.

I stuck my swords up, making an X. Then my swords started

to glow, and it fired a blast. Jonah immediately drew his spear. It started to spark in lightning. Vincent pulled an arrow out and shot it. Before it could reach me, I sliced it in half. I charged and jumped. When I was close to hitting the ground, I put my fist out and created a shock wave. Jonah and Vincent went flying and hit their backs on a rock.

"Max!" Cindy yelled. "We're sorry, and if we really hurt your feelings, we are really sorry."

"Sorry doesn't cut!" I yelled back angrily. I made my swords glow light blue. I felt the power I had.

I ran really fast and attacked Cindy very hard. It seemed as if I had super strength and speed. I lifted my hands, and water from the rivers and lakes rose to my power. I then sent the water flying at my friends. When the water cleared up, I saw my friends sitting there, beaten up and tired. Jonah got up and created another spark on his spear.

"You should know your science, Max," Jonah said, smiling.

"What's so funny?" I replied.

He ran with weariness and yelled, "Water is highly conductive of electricity." When he was close, I made a block of earth come up from the ground and hit him, but he used that to jump. As he was coming down, the bolt of electricity became larger and larger. Then there was nothing left for me to do, so I decided to take the hit. It was more painful than I thought it would be. I fell to the ground, holding my stomach. Jonah kept hitting me over and over.

"Do you give up!" he yelled.

After that, I drop kicked him, and then he fell. We both got up at the same time. Both our weapons were ready. We ran toward each other and battled out with our weapons. It was kind of like a light saber battle of Star Wars. I tried to remember the counter attack Blaze did, then I remembered. I waited until Jonah attacked, then I placed one sword to block it. Then I did a back flip kick, and he fell.

Out of nowhere, an arrow blew up on my back. I could feel the burn on my back. When I turned, Vincent was aiming another arrow at me. He shot it, and I tried to cut it in half, but it blew up in big fog of ice. Before you knew it, I was frozen in an ice cube. After a while, Vincent kept launching regular bomb arrows, but I was still frozen when Jonah regained himself, and he got his spear ready. Vincent nodded his head and shot an unfamiliar arrow. When it was close, Jonah threw his spear while it was charged with static. At that moment, the ice melted, but it was too late. When it touched me, one thousand ultrasonic waves mixed together with deadly electricity created the most devastating attack ever. I fell to the ground and passed out.

It felt as if days had passed. I woke up beside a cabin fire. I looked up, and it was dark. Then I saw all my friends sleeping except for Vincent.

He looked at me and said, "You're awake."

"Vincent, why are you awake?" I asked.

"All of us agreed to take shifts to be on guard and watch you," he replied.

"After all this trouble I put you all through, you'll still want me to be your friend?" I asked. He said yes firmly.

He turned around and grabbed a small-sized yellow bottle.

"When did you all get sleeping bags?" I asked.

"We bought it in a magical convenient store along with other useful items we needed for camping," he replied.

He opened the bottle and put it to my mouth and said, "Drink up." When I drank it, it filled a good sensation in my mouth.

"Good," I replied.

"Well, you won't have any more of those," he said.

"Why?" I questioned.

"Because it can kill if you take too much of it."

"Oh!" I said, feeling stupid.

"You should get some more sleep," Vincent said firmly.

I closed my eyes and slept. Suddenly, I saw myself on top of a balcony. I looked beat up and stomped on. I also saw another figure standing on another balcony.

"Let's finish this!" the figure roared. Then my dream shifted. I was in Black Hand's headquarters.

Zemnas was talking to me.

"This is your destiny to stay with us!" he yelled.

"I'm leaving this organization," I said.

"You can't do this without getting through me," he replied. Zemnas jumped off his high chair and fast wind started to circle me.

"You'll never win," he commented.

I tried to even out the wind with water, but the wind kept canceling it out. Suddenly, the wind began to move rapidly and started a tornado. After a while, it flew me across the room.

He walked closer and said, "I told you that it is your destiny."

"No, it's not!" I yelled.

I grabbed my sword and tried to slice him, but the wind sliced my sword instead. He choked me by my throat and lifted me up.

"This is your destiny."

Suddenly, I woke up. I saw everyone packing up to go. Cindy was packing my stuff too. I stood up and said, "Are we almost ready?"

"Who dropped dead and made you the leader?" Cindy replied. I smiled, knowing she was playing.

I went over to Vincent and Jonah and asked them, "How did you make that attack?"

"We practiced it for hours and didn't master completely. We just fired the attack to see whether it would work," Vincent explained.

"Done!" Cindy and Clair shouted.

"Good job, now let's get going," Jonah replied.

"So where do we go?" I asked curiously.

Jonah dug in his pocket and said, "We have a map."

"Where did you get it?" I asked.

Jonah replied, "The guy at the train station gave it to us."

I looked at the map and saw a big map that included water.

"First, we go straight and make a right," Jonah directed.

As we walked, Vincent said that we were lucky that, at Mountain of Peace, there weren't any monsters. But he jinxed it. We started hearing noises in the nearby bushes and crackling in the trees.

"I see you," a voice whispered.

Vincent turned around, pulled an arrow out of his quiver, and shot it in the sky. Suddenly, everything fell out of the trees and bushes. The things that fell out were insects, fruits, bypassing animals, and leaves. Twigs and stumps were the only things left.

"Vincent!" Cindy yelled. "Why did you do that?"

"To see whether something was following us," he replied determined. When we walked farther, something grabbed Cindy out of the bushes. "Ah!" she screamed.

Vincent, Jonah, and I took out our weapons and attacked. A few minutes after, we kept attacking, the hand went back into the bushes.

We helped Cindy up and asked her, "Are you okay?"

"Sure," she replied, scared.

Then a figure jumped out of the same bushes; it was Ron.

"Why won't you die?" I yelled fiercely.

"Cindy and Clair, fall back while Jonah, Vincent, and I take care of this crybaby."

"Crybaby!" Ron yelled.

Ron looked more torn apart than ever. Almost all his hair were gone, all his face was scorched, his right eyeball was gone, and his clothes were tattered. He made two big fireballs in his hands and threw them. All of us jumped out of the way. He winked his left eye and purple fire surrounded all of us.

"Can't run away this time," Ron chuckled.

Vincent fired a freeze arrow, but Ron broke right through. Jonah jammed his spear in the ground and electricity sparked Ron's feet. He seemed not to be affected. In the blink of an eye, he was already in front of Jonah and Vincent. He hit both of them in the chest with his elbow while doing a 360-degree spin and slammed both of them in the ground.

He walked closer to me and said, "You children have bothered me long enough."

"You're the one following us, trying to kill us," I replied. "Oh, and how did you know where we were?"

"Your slimy little spy informs me every time."

I used my powers to make one big tsunami wave.

He looked to his sides and said, "Not this again." He ran and was in front of my face. Then he took one good blow in my stomach. I fell to the ground, holding my stomach in pain. Luckily, I didn't pass out. I saw Clair sneaking up behind Ron with a stick. My vision was foggy, but I saw Clair hit Ron in the head, and he fell. When Vincent and Jonah got up, we all started attacking Ron uncontrollably. When he started to wake up, he was scorched in fire. When he screamed for mercy, he blew up in a big bang. The ground he blew up in was a deep ditch with cracks.

It was already noon, but we decided to keep walking. As we walked, we discussed. "If we killed Ron twice, how come he came back a third time?", I asked.

"Because when you're resurrected from Tartarus, you're granted with extra powers, but I don't know how he came back again", Cindy said.

We saw a nearby cavern and decided to sleep there. Jonah stayed to guard. Somehow, I couldn't sleep. I just looked at the stars all night. I thought about my mom and the dad that I never met. I also thought about Kronos being my grandfather. Then I thought about a major part of our journey—the traitor. I knew the spy had to know where we were going the whole time. So I know the only person that we called to inform where we were was Drake. But Drake could have told Chiron while somebody's eavesdropping to tell the whole of Magic School. How could the traitor send all those people to distract us from our mission? I asked myself. I remembered what Barbus told Cindy and me. "It's someone you trust the most." Who do I trust the most? I asked myself. My mom. But she's my mother, and she's never been in Magic School long enough to betray everybody. I thought of everyone else that could be capable of being a traitor. Grace. But she is the daughter of Zeus; she couldn't possibly be the traitor. Lucas, that sneaky slimeball. He's fast enough, smart enough, and sneaky enough. I can't judge him yet because I don't really know him that well. I thought of everyone in Magic School. When I tried to narrow down, I realized how sleepy I was, and I dozed off. When I woke up, I saw all my friends sleeping, including Jonah who was supposed to be the guard.

I got up, grabbed my book bag, and left the cavern to explore Mountain of Peace. I grabbed nearby stones and dug them into the ground as I walked so I could leave a trail. When I reached a forest that looked somehow like a jungle, from a distance, I saw a gigantic river. I ran to it and dipped my hands in it and drank some water. It was so fresh. It made bottled water seem like tap water.

When I looked up, I saw a lion drinking water as well. It also looked at me fiercely. It leaped over the water at me. It sunk its claws into my leg as I tried to run. When it tattered my clothes up, it let go. Then I saw myself bleeding uncontrollably. I started following the trail that I left and was almost at the cavern. As I ran, I could hear the growling of the lion chasing me. When I reached the cavern, it jumped and tried to bite me again.

"Wake up!" I yelled at my friends.

I ran toward Cindy's sleeping bag, and she woke up screaming. The lion stopped and purred like a kitten. Cindy groomed it and scratched behind its ear. The lion purred again softly. "Where did all that blood come from," she asked.

"It was the lion," I said, and at that time, Vincent jumped up and immediately stopped the bleeding. Then he put some liquid he squeezed out of the surrounding leaves. It healed, and the pains were gone.

"There, kitty, kitty," Cindy said. The lion lay down and closed its eyes. "Max! What are you thinking bringing a three-hundred-pound lion here?"

"It followed me," I replied.

"We can keep it as a pet," Cindy said.

When the rest of my friends woke up, they were mad and surprised but allowed Cindy to keep it. We were all ready to move out.

Jonah pulled out the map and said, "This way." He pointed in the same direction I'd left a trail.

"I know the way!" I yelled as I ran toward the trail. Everybody followed me. "This is where I got the lion."

Suddenly, a purple portal appeared. Blaze came out.

"For now, you are not a full member," he said, disappointed.

The robe they gave me teleported out of my book bag. He then walked back into the portal and left. "Who was he?" Jonah asked.

"No one," I replied secretively.

We walked farther into the jungle. We saw villagers farming crops into the ground. Scattered beside them were potatoes, peppers, cassavas, cocoyams, yams, and corn. There was also under a tree an old laid-back man wearing blue overalls and a yellow hat, sitting on a haystack chair, drinking palm wine, and eating coconut and tapioca. I felt hungry, but then I remembered what my mother told me—not to eat food from strangers.

"Yes! I'm starving!" Vincent yelled and ran to the man. The rest of my friends followed and so did I.

"What's your name, sir?" Jonah asked.

"Josiah's the name," the old man said with a country accent. "Now, what're you kids doing in this part of the mountain?"

"We are trying to find Ezinna," I replied.

"You're far from there, I reckon," he said.

"But we are here to get some food from you," Vincent added. I hit him with my elbow for being rude.

"Bet you kids are hungry," he said generously.

"Starving," Vincent said.

"Betty!" the old man yelled.

"Sir!" a woman yelled from the back. Then from behind the house, beside the tree that Josiah was sitting under, an elderly woman popped out.

"We got some visitors," the woman said.

"Kids, meet my wife, Betty." She also had a country accent. She wore a dusty red-checkered dress. "Fix some potatoes with the usual spiced stew, stat!" Josiah yelled.

She ran back behind the house, then Cindy and I went as

well. Clair, Jonah, and Vincent were too busy listening to Josiah's ridiculous "back when I was a boy" speech. Betty pounded the tomatoes and put sliced-up red peppers in the bowl that she pounded tomatoes in. After that, she went to the kettle and poured hot water while stirring it. When she finished fixing the stew, she boiled potatoes. After she was done cooking, I said, "It smells good."

"Notin' special," she replied. "I always fix this for my husband."

While Betty, Cindy, and I were going out of the backyard, we noticed everybody was already inside the house preparing for dinner. When I looked outside, I saw the lion sleeping. We all prayed and ate our food.

Surprisingly, that was the best home-cooked meal I'd ever had. Matter of fact, that was the only home-cooked meal I'd ever had. Because you know, New York is a busy place where people don't have time to cook at home. When I finished, I thanked her for the food and went back outside and waited for the others. In about ten minutes, my friends finished and came outside. The old couple also came outside and asked us, "Leaving so soon?"

"Um! Yes, ma'am, we are quite in a hurry," Jonah replied.

When we walked, Josiah yelled, "Now you kids have a safe trip."

Cindy walked toward the lion and said, "Come on, big guy, we have to go." The lion woke up happily and followed us.

"I think we should name him Dan," Vincent suggested. Cindy put her hand on her chin and thought about it for a second.

"Dan will do," she replied.

When we walked out to the jungle, we pulled out the map. Jonah put his finger on our location and dragged it to a nearby city. "Maybe here we can get some clues on where to go," Jonah said. The walk was long and hard, but we managed. We were at least two hundred miles from the town.

"It's getting dark, and I think we should camp out here for the night," Jonah said.

Clair blew the inflatable tent, and everybody got in. We all made our sleeping bags and slept, except for me. I snuggled out and unzipped Clair's backpack. I grabbed the magical book on information for anything magical. I took it back in my sleeping bag and zipped it to a point where I could still breathe. I turned on the flashlight I got from my backpack. I looked up Black Hand. The book was kind of like a dictionary; it was organized from A-Z. I found it, and it read, "The Black Hand is a ruthless organization that looks for powerful demigods to help them fulfill their ultimate goal: slaughtering every single god there is and gaining their power, also granting every member with power, making them slowly invincible." I gasped and thought in mind what kind of person would do this.

I got out of my sleeping bag and went out of the tent with the book. There was more reading in the book, and I urged myself to keep reading. I sat down on the grass and read. "There are fourteen members in total. The leader is known as Zemnas, son of the wind god Aeolus. He is strong in power and can control wind."

If I join the Black Hand, I'll be an enemy of my dad, I thought in my mind. I read even more.

"If one were to betray the organization, they would be destroyed." For some odd reason, I wasn't scared.

"Max, are you okay?" Cindy said while coming out.

"No, but you promise to keep a secret," I replied.

"Of course, what is it?" she said.

"You remember that guy that came and talked to me that was dressed in a black robe?"

"Yeah, so?"

"He was a member of the Black Hand."

"What! Why? Are you involved with them?"

"I'm actually a partial member, but I only joined them because I was mad."

"Max, do you understand the danger of being part of them?"

"No, I don't, why?"

"If the gods found out, you could get killed. The reason is, why would you join an organization that destroys gods to get power?"

I shrugged my shoulders.

"Okay, I'll tell you the story of how the Black Hand came to be.

"Aeolus, the wind god, was sitting down on his thrown, talking to fellow gods when his demigod son Zemnas walked in the room Aeolus was in. Zemnas, a healthy adult, never knew his father since birth until he was thirteen. His mother finally told him who his father was.

"Zemnas's scent was so strong that it attracted thousands of monsters. Every time monsters chased him, he prayed to his father, hoping he could help him. When he was nineteen, his father gave his mother an amulet to give to Zemnas. The amulet made Zemnas immortal. Zemnas discovered his powers shortly after. Darkness slowly consumed Zemnas's heart and made him angry. He wanted revenge on every monster that tried to eat and kill him. So he planned to destroy all of them, and he did. He nearly put monsters to extinction.

"He thought more about his childhood and wanted revenge on his father for not helping him when monsters tried to eat him. He asked his mother how to get to Olympus, and she told him. Once he got to Olympus, he searched for Aeolus. When Zeus stopped him and asked him why he was there, he replied rudely and said, 'None of your business.'

"Zeus attacked him with a thunderbolt, but Zemnas blew the attack away and ran. He busted and threw nearby doors. Luckily, Aeolus was there.

"Aeolus turned to Zemnas and asked, 'Who are you?'

"'You didn't even care to know what I looked like. I'm your son!' Zemnas yelled sharply. 'I believed in you, and you didn't even care whether I was dead or not. I'm here to destroy you!'

"Aeolus laughed loudly.

"'Ahhh!' Zemnas shouted. Zemnas jumped and created a wind barrier that shielded him and kept him in the air. Zemnas then used his hands to unleash strong winds at Aeolus.

"'That tickled,' Aeolus chuckled.

"'You think I'm playing!'" Zemnas shouted.

"'Please, son, I can kill you in one second,' Aeolus replied.

"'I'd like to see you try,' Zemnas demanded.

"'I knew that woman couldn't raise you well,' Aeolus mumbled.

"'Couldn't raise me well,' Zemnas said. 'You were never in my life!'

"'I couldn't claim you at that time!' Aeolus unleashed tornadoes just by shouting once.

"Zemnas flew and hit his back hard on a wall. Zemnas got up, enraged. He flew up in the sky and shouted. He started to channel his power immensely with powerful winds surrounding him. Zemnas flew to Aeolus's face and punched him a few times. Aeolus grabbed him and squeezed him tightly.

"'You're not dead,' Aeolus said.

"'I'm immortal, you idiot,' Zemnas replied.

"'Oh, that amulet I gave to you.'

"More anger flew through Zemnas's body. Zemnas blew hard on Aeolus's face. Aeolus squeezed Zemnas tighter.

"'You really think you can beat me,' Aeolus bluffed.

"'I'm gonna kill you!' Zemnas shouted loudly.

"Aeolus threw Zemnas to the wall, but Zemnas gained balance using his powers. Zemnas used his hands to make strong winds rush at high speed. The winds were so strong and fast that it broke all the nearby windows.

"'Nice one, son,' Aeolus joked.

"'You won't be laughing at your death, you old man!' Zemnas yelled.

"'Reason I'm laughing is because you can't kill a god,' Aeolus said.

"'Then I'll be the first,' Zemnas replied. Zemnas knew that you could weaken a god's power by destroying their throne. Zemnas used wind to completely remove all the thrones except for the one Aeolus was sitting in from the ground. He used them to hit Aeolus. Aeolus then rose from his throne.

"'Ahhhh!' Zemnas shouted once more. But this time the wind

that he summoned became black. The wind surrounded Aeolus like a tornado and swirled him away from his throne. Zemnas made wind come within the chair and totally destroyed Aeolus's throne.

"'Uhh!' Aeolus said in pain.

"'Heh,' Zemnas chuckled because he weakened Aeolus. Zemnas created a giant wind hand and choked Aeolus. 'Now I told you I was going to kill you.'

"'I love you, son,' Aeolus huffed.

"'Don't use flattery now,' Zemnas shouted. Zemnas used the wind hand and lifted Aeolus up. He then threw Aeolus to the ground. Zemnas saw Ares's spear and picked it up.

"'You can't use that spear because it's rude to use another god's weapon without permission,' Aeolus said.

"'Don't care,' Zemnas replied.

Zemnas used force to stab Aeolus in the chest. Instantly, Aeolus died under Zemnas's hand. Zeus looked at Zemnas in amazement.

"How could a demigod defeat a god? Zeus thought in his head.

"Zemnas turned around and said, 'Mission accomplished.' Wind rushed from the sky, and Zemnas was gone.

"When Zemnas arrived at his house, he thought, Why not kill every god to get power? Zemnas found every way he could to fulfill his purpose, and he did. He discovered a giant sacred stone tablet with fifty hands connecting to it. The ancient Titans used it when they killed a fellow Titan in a rivalry to gain their powers. But you'd have to transmit the powers when they are in an orb."

"Where do they get the orb?" I asked Cindy.

"I don't know, but let me finish the story," she replied. "Once the power is in the orb, you must place the orb on the hand of the stone tablet. When all the hands are filled with orbs, the world will be the Black Hand's. But let's backtrack on how he got members. He searched for valuable, strong, and worthy demigods to recruit. If one joins the Black Hand, they instantly become immortal. He magnified the power of the amulet his father gave him to put on members, which also make them immortal. He sends those members to do the dirty work, meaning destroying the gods."

I hesitated and thought about why they choose me. "Do you know anything about two members that I met named Xemas and Blaze?"

She broke in shock. "So you do know what," I said.

"Blaze is the son of Haphaestus, and Xemas is the son of Erebus, god of darkness."

"I thought Hades was the god of darkness," I said.

"Hades is the god of the underworld and way much stronger and important. But don't let Erebus's minority fool you. Xemas is way stronger than you think. There are more members that I know, but it's not the time to explain."

"What do you mean it's not the time to explain!" I yelled.

Cindy calmed me down and whispered, "Zeus only told me, Chiron, and the rest of the gods that sooner or later, Black Hand will come after the Olympians, and they will be powerless."

"Powerless," I replied.

"Yeah, if one demigod was able to take out one god then a couple demigods are able to take out Zeus."

"Where do they get the power?" I asked.

"Well, they haven't made their final move, but they will, and the gods don't know what they're up against. All I know is that Zemnas has all Aeolus's powers, plus his own."

"Have they taken out any gods to consume power?" I asked.

"Only one," she replied.

"Who?"

"That's the only thing I can't tell you," she said.

I looked up in the sky, and it was already morning. "We should get going," I suggested.

"You better not tell anybody about the information I gave you," she added. She went in the tent and prepared.

By the time I went to go get my backpack, she was already done. I woke everybody up including the lion, which was hard.

"What a coincidence," Vincent said.

"What?" Jonah replied.

"There's a store right there, which means we are already close to the main city town."

"Great," I said.

Clair went in the store and asked them where Ezinna's Palace was. When we all went in, the man said that it's a long way if we were not familiar with Mountain of Peace.

"Just give us the directions," she demanded.

The man pulled out a medium-sized map. "Take it," he offered. We walked out and continued our journey.

I took out the mirror and tried to call Chiron.

"Hello," Chiron answered.

"Finally!" I screamed.

"So where are you kids now?" Chiron asked.

"We are on Mountain of Peace," I replied. "You guys are already there?"

"Yeah, we've been trying to contact you, but Drake kept answering and saying you're busy," I said.

"Are you sure? Because I've been in my office the whole time," he replied.

"We have a lot to tell you when we get back, but for now, we have to get going," I finally told Chiron.

"I'll see you when you get back," he said.

He signed off, and I thought why Drake would tell a lie. I tried to get that off my mind and focused on the mission.

Clair was looking at the map and said, "These directions are confusing, and I'm the daughter of Athena."

"Don't flatter yourself," Jonah said rudely. Clair looked at him as if he was crazy.

"That's something Vincent would've said," Clair replied.

"Hey!" Vincent yelled because of what Clair said.

"It is true," I added.

"All of you just stop it!" Cindy screamed. All of a sudden, everything got quiet.

"You guys need to stop arguing and find a solution," Cindy said and snatched the map from Clair and looked at it.

"It was backwards," she said when she finished. "I'm going

to be leading this trip for now." As she walked, we followed. Before we knew it, we were already in a forest.

"This is a village area," Clair said.

We saw little huts with haystack roofs. Also, a middle-aged woman with a baby tied to her back came out a hut. Suddenly, a man with a spear came in front of us with more men with spears behind him.

"Who are you people?" the man that led the other men asked. The man had three scars over his eye that seemed to have no pupil. He was shirtless with a lion's paw print on his left chest. He also had on dark green capri and was barefooted.

"My name is Cindy, and these are my friends," she replied.

The man growled. "Are you intimidated by my lion?" Cindy asked him.

"Most definitely not!" he shouted. "My name is General Scar." General Scar looked over Cindy and said, "Jonah, is that you?"

"You know Jonah?" Cindy asked.

"Silence. I did not give you permission to speak," General Scar said to Cindy.

"Hey, General Scar," Jonah said unhappily.

"Just because you left this village for two years doesn't mean you can now disrespect me. You need to address me with respect!" General Scar yelled at Jonah.

Jonah looked mad and pulled out his spear.

"Still think you can challenge me," General Scar chuckled. Jonah withdrew his spear and bowed down to General Scar. "That's more like it," General Scar said.

"Who do you think you are! Telling my friend to show more respect," I yelled.

"Max!" Jonah yelled at me surprisingly.

"Obviously, you have no respect for people," General Scar said to me harshly.

"No, you don't have respect for anyone, and I'm challenging you to a duel," I replied. How stupid, I thought in my head.

"Good," he said. "A duel means we can't use any weapons

and also no restrictions."

"Meaning?" I asked.

"Last man standing," he said superiorly.

Suddenly, the men that followed him started to set a straw cage.

I positioned like a boxer. How am I going to win without my sword? I said to myself. "Begin!" a man yelled.

General Scar charged like a lion. I ran out of the way, and he hit his head on the cage. I then figured something out quickly. That he's very reckless when attacking. I formulated a plan slowly. He charged again, but this time, he made a big turn and foiled my plans. When he turned, he grabbed me in a headlock. He almost suffocated me to death. Then he threw me straight into the opposite side of the cage. I didn't know how to beat this guy. I then remembered that he said no weapons but said nothing about powers. I transferred water from a nearby lake and splashed him with impact. The odd thing about it was the water was cold, and he ran after me without any sign of getting hit.

"I don't know what you just did, but I'm still going to kick your butt," he said. When he got his hands out, I saw his nails, and they were like a bear's claws. When I ran toward him, he tried to scratch me, but I dodged and grabbed his arm. After that, I twisted it and got him down to the floor by pinning him on the back.

"Say you give up!" I yelled at the general.

"Never," he replied.

I twisted it harder and he yelled, "Ahhh! Okay."

"Yes!" I yelled victoriously. I quickly got off of him and went to the edge of the cage. "Open up, I won."

"No, boy, last man standing," General Scar said viciously.

He ran behind me and grabbed me by the neck sinking his claws into my throat. He threw me to the other side of the cage and punched me on the face. Blood flooded down my mouth. He then grabbed me by the head and nearly crushed my skull. When I was on the floor, he scratched me in the chest and arms a couple of times. He pushed his foot in my chest, and I passed out.

I woke up in a hut with Jonah looking over me. My shirt was off, and I had bandages wrapped from my chest to my stomach. Little bandages covered my small scars.

"What you did was dumb," Jonah said to me.

"Heh!" I said.

"General Scar has been trained in those cages since he was five and never lost, and he wasn't going to lose to a twelve-year-old," he added.

"What happened to his eye?" I asked.

"No one is allowed to talk about that, but try asking General Scar himself."

"You're right, no one is allowed to talk about it," someone said behind the hut. General Scar came in, and Jonah left.

General Scar walked over to me and asked, "Do you really want to know what happened to my eye?"

"Yeah," I replied.

"Thirty years ago, there was an invasion from the British. They killed everyone important to me, including my parents. When they were done, they sent watchdogs to search the area for any remaining people and jewelry. I was dumb enough to try to take on one of their dogs. Then it sunk its claws into my eye, and I was scarred for life as well as the loss of my eye."

"I'm sorry," I said.

"Sorry won't bring back my parents," he replied.

I actually felt sorry for a guy that almost killed me. I looked at my shirt and wanted to wear it, but it was filled with mud and dirt from all the times I fell. I tried to get up, but my legs were sore. I just lay down and thought about the trip. It was hard, and it's not yet even a fighting mission. Who knows how bad the fighting mission would be. I forced myself to get up, and I did. My shirt was too dirty to wear, so I just went shirtless outside.

"Max!" Jonah yelled as he came to me. "You're too hurt."

"We should really get going," I replied.

"I know, but since your wounds are still vulnerable, we should stay a day and rest," he said gladly.

"No, we are leaving now," I demanded.

I went to General Scar and asked him whether he had an extra shirt my size.

"Sure," he replied.

He went in one of the huts and brought back a black shirt with one big blue wolf in the middle. When I put it on, it was a muscle shirt and comfortable. I picked up my backpack and got the group together.

Jonah was clearly defiant of not leaving, but we took a vote, and he lost. So we moved on, and he followed.

"Bye! Bye!" the villagers yelled at us.

"Bye!" we replied back.

We walked farther into the forest.

Suddenly, we saw a little girl and a little, but older boy plucking oranges with a sharp knife.

"Hey! Where are your parents!" I yelled to them.

"Max, here in Mountain of Peace, children don't need to be supervised to go anywhere they want," Jonah said.

"You people, you guys look hungry and tired, who are you?" the girl said to us.

"We are in a hurry to get somewhere," I replied.

"Where?" she asked.

"Ezinna's Palace Village Estate," I said.

"My father's name is Ezinna," she replied. "Is it my father you have come to see?"

"Yes, if it the same Ezinna," I said.

"No way," Vincent said happily and surprisingly too.

"You are lying," I said fiercely.

"No! It is true that I am the daughter of Ezinna you have come to see." The girl was dressed in a clean brown T-shirt with tan short shorts. "Carol!" a voice yelled.

Then a boy started to come out the woods. The boy had tan shorts and no shirt on. There were three hunting knives attached to a utility belt also with a portable water canteen. I guessed there would be water in the canteen.

"Leave my sister alone!" the boy yelled.

The boy seemed to be nine and was our height.

"Don't worry, Felix. These people are here to see our father," Carol said.

"What do you want with our father?" the boy asked.

"We want to ask him whether we could use part of his estate."

"What do you want with my father's estate?"

"To help this village against your dad's enemies."

Then he looked at me with sorrow. "I'm sorry for harassing you, my name is Felix, and this is my sister, Carol," he replied. "But who are you and where are you from?

"I'm Max," I said.

"I'm Jonah."

"I'm Cindy."

"I'm Vincent."

"And I'm Clair."

"We are from America, and we have come to see Ezinna," I chipped in. "Let me take you to the palace and introduce you to my dad."

CHAPTER 10

❋

EZINNA TAKEN BY SURPRISE

As we walked, Felix led the group while cutting weeds that were in the way. From a distance, I could see Ezinna's Palace.

"We are almost there," Felix added.

When we were close to the palace, there was a gate with a man next to it. As I looked around, I saw many guards pointing their guns at us ready to shoot.

"It's okay!" Felix yelled.

The guards lowered their guns and stood back into position.

"Open the gates," Felix told the man.

"Who are these people?" the men at the gates asked in unison.

"My friends," Felix replied.

"Your father won't be happy," one said.

We all walked into the premises. The palace was huge. Eight nice, clean, and new cars were parked on the front lot. I also saw another car, my favorite, a red Lamborghini parked underneath a mango tree.

"All of these are your father's?" I asked Felix.

"Yeah," he said happily.

When he opened the front door, I saw a big living room. The

TV was a flat screen. There were four sofa sets that were green leather.

"Let's take the elevator," Felix said.

"Seriously," I replied.

He turned to the right and led to the staircase. Next to it was a metal elevator. Felix pressed one of the buttons, and it opened. We all entered, and Carol pressed five.

"There is a fifth floor?" Clair asked.

"Well, kinda," Carol replied.

In one minute, we were there. When we appeared in a palace, I knew we were going to see Ezinna. Then we walked farther in, and we saw shirtless guards everywhere with spears. When I looked up, I saw an old man with a red cap, traditional yellow African chieftaincy regalia, and gold sandals. Behind him on the wall were lion and tiger skins, which I guessed showed that he had killed many animals before. In front of him was a stool. Sitting on it was a plate of rice with stew and chicken. The old man was eating it without noticing us as we entered.

Felix bowed down to the old man and said, "Father, I've brought you some friends of mine that want to see you."

"What!" the man yelled back like he did not hear him well.

"These people have come to see you, Father!" Felix yelled back, and he bowed again.

"Oh!" he replied as if he did not hear well.

"That's Ezinna?" I asked surprisingly.

Cindy hit me in the chest and bowed down as well as my other friends. After a while, so did I.

"What are you kids here for and where are you from?" Ezinna asked with eyes open in absolute surprise. And he said again, "What you kids want in this palace?"

I was kinda overwhelmed. This place was imposing. So instead of talking, I decided to take out the mirror to see whether Chiron would explain. I knocked on the mirror, and Chiron answered.

"What is it, Max?" Chiron asked respectively.

"Talk to Ezinna about what you need," I replied.

I lifted the mirror to Ezinna. Then he took a hard look at me and turned to see and listen. "Ezinna, long time no see," Chiron said.

"Chiron, is that you?"

"Yes, sir," Chiron replied in humility.

I turned the mirror to face myself, and I asked, "Chiron, how do you know Ezinna?"

Chiron replied, "We first met in Philosophy School, and we became very close friends. Ezinna told me he was going back to his country and going to remain in his place as king. Right before his flight, I told him everything about Greek mythology, magic, and the gods. Unlike any other mortal, he remained calm and stable. Two years later, he called me from Nigeria and asked me to be his best man at his wedding. From that time, I knew he was going to be a reliable friend. I was there for his first baby naming ceremony. Anyway, let me talk to Ezinna," he instructed.

I turned the mirror back to Ezinna, and Chiron began to speak. "Ezinna, I'm sorry to bother you, but there is something big going to happen. I need part of your estate for a medical camp and also a reinforcement area for a future war."

"And I benefit from this how?" Ezinna asked.

"I've done some more research on your village, and I know that one of your enemies' villages and the bad foreigners want to destroy your village, so the children that I sent are going to help you fight. They are preparing to attack and wipe out your whole village and your estate."

"What!" I yelled. "That was never part of the mission."

"Max, drastic times call for drastic measures," Chiron replied.

"Deal!" Ezinna also said.

"Good," Chiron said, and he signed off.

"Before we start anything, get these guests nourishments," Ezinna told one of the guards.

The guard walked to the door, and all of us stopped bowing and followed. Then we walked out of the palace with the guard to follow him to the main dining room. In the dining room, there were two long tables with white cloths. On the right table were metal plates covered with metal covers.

"Choices are there for you to take," the guard said. All of us went nearer to the fruit basket and sat down.

"We have to build up strength to fight," I told my friends. In about ten minutes, we were done.

I went to Ezinna and asked him, "When do we fight?"

"Whenever they strike, but I might also want to be at peace with them," he replied. "This region is called Mountain of Peace, and we don't want any more wars."

"So what do we do for the meantime?"

"Anything," he replied. "I'm going to call the Council of Elders and the wise men of the land to ask them any suggestions about this threat."

I was already bored and didn't want to do anything. I wanted to go back to Magic School or do a different mission.

"Guards!" Ezinna yelled loudly. "Summon General Scar and the Council of Elders to the village square five o'clock in the morning."

"Yes, sir!" the guards yelled back in respect, and off they went.

"Max, maybe you should meet up with your friends," Ezinna told me.

"I will," I replied back and left.

I saw Felix and my friends. While Vincent, Jonah, and Clair were watching TV, I saw Cindy talking to Felix. When I walked to them, I asked them, "What should we do?"

"Well, Cindy and I are going to walk around the village to know more about it. Want to come?" he asked me.

"Sure," I replied, and we were ready to go.

Chapter 11

The Insight

As we went out the gate, the gateman asked, "Where are you going now, Felix?"

"Nowhere special, just show my friends around," he replied.

When we were back in the forest, Felix mumbled, "Pain in the butt," for some reason. As we walked farther into the forest, we were in a square-shaped surface. The area was huge and had a stage along with two bleachers.

"This is the village square," Felix said. "This is where important events and meetings take place."

We took a right turn and saw a big ranch house the size of a three-story house.

"This is where my mother cooks, cleans, and rests. Through the back, it leads straight into my father's palace."

A few seconds later, an elderly woman with a gray T-shirt and a long skirt waved at Felix.

"Who is that?" I asked Felix.

"That's my mom," he replied.

"Felix, who are those people?" his mom asked.

"They're my friends, and they are here to help my father."

Felix's mother came closer and introduced herself. She

had fluorescent hazel eyes, and her hair came to her shoulders. At close range, she looked light tan and much younger than I thought, and she was beautiful. I wondered what she looked like at my age.

"My name is Gladys," she said.

"My name is Max, and this is my friend, Cindy."

"It's nice to meet you," she said delightfully.

"You're here to help us handle the foreigners?" she asked us.

"Yes, ma'am," I replied.

Then she looked up in a sudden deep thought, and she looked down on us and said, "You guys have a safe walk," while she walked back toward the ranch.

"What is she doing?" I asked Felix.

"Oh! She's just preparing dinner."

"Anyway, let's continue the walk," I demanded.

When we made a right turn, there was a round table with four old men sitting down and discussing about economics and how to help the village.

"Shhh!" Felix whispered. "This is the table where the Council of Elders meet and talk."

"So this is where your dad is going to discuss about the foreigners?" I asked quietly.

"Yeah, I guess so," he replied. "These people are having a meeting right now. I think we should go somewhere else."

Felix, Cindy, and I quietly crept to the left, and it lead into another village. Then we saw another group of people inside the forest.

"Uh-oh!" Felix said to himself.

"What is it?" Cindy said.

"I'm not familiar with those people and this village too," he replied, worried.

"Instead of running back, let's try to introduce ourselves to them," I said.

When I was about to get up and walk, Felix grabbed me by the shirt and pulled me back.

"You don't understand. This is an enemy village," he told me, frightened. "We must hide, and they must never see us, or they will kill us."

Then we hid behind a large tree not too far away where we could hear everything they said in whispering voices. We listened.

"You know, we have to show Ezinna," the huge bearded man said. "He does not realize that our villages have been enemies for years. We are just going along until we are ready to fight back, and the time is now. If we do not get him this time, it will be hard for us."

Another suggested that since they knew and were working with the bad foreigners to try to give Ezinna a bad deal, they would join at the same time to make trouble for him so that their village would be the leader of them too.

The tall man in shirt and tie and cap warned them against the plan because in his mind Ezinna was too much. "He went to a philosophy school in an oversea country, and he has big connections everywhere. His friends are top government people and military people and police people. He is a wise man. Not only that, Ezinna has tried to make peace, and he did not make trouble for anybody in our village since he became king and since he was a child. All that he is worried about is that we send our people to school like he did all his people, and he is a faithful Christian. God will not be happy with us if we hurt such an innocent good man," the man told them. "I will not be a party to such an unjust attack. I do not want bloodshed in our village and in Mountain of Peace.

"So you want us to keep serving under him?" the dark man said after being quiet for so long.

"No!" the tall man said. "All we should do is, first, train our people for the next ten years, and then send an emissary to Ezinna so we can be in peace and also ask that we have our own king still out of Mountain of Peace. He is a good man, and I am sure he will not refuse."

The bearded man was determined, and it looked as if he had a lot of influence on the others, and he persuaded them that they must attack Ezinna by surprise when he did not expect it. Before they dispersed, the huge bearded man pulled out a handgun and shot the tall man in tie. The huge bearded man laughed while watching him die. The dark man looked at the dead man in guiltiness, felt uneasy, and walked away. Then the other two walked away instead, in the opposite directions, leaving the dead man there.

Cindy and I did not like what we heard and saw. Felix was scared as if he was about to scream, but we shut our mouth and tiptoed ourselves, walking farther down before we turned round back to the palace side.

"What do we do now, Felix?" I asked

"Nothing," Felix said, "but we should tell my father what we just heard and saw, where we heard it, and describe the people to him. I am sure he will know what to do."

"Let's go, I am hungry," Cindy demanded. As we walked, we felt sad for the man who died. I also was scared of what might happen at the meeting between Ezinna and the foreigners. I kind of lightened up, thinking that this village was strong in all kinds of ways. Then I became happy thinking about Ezinna's influence on everybody. Felix was not happy; he was devastated to see a man killed who was trying to stand up for his father. He was not even part of this village and we wondered what the bearded man might do to an ordinary villager who is.

Cindy held hands with Felix to cheer him up. As we walked, Felix was so sad that he did not duck or walk around the overgrown leaves that were hitting his face. At that time, I felt like an outcast, knowing that I was just there to help and that Felix was emotionally attached to the ongoing feud that was happening. There and then, I realized that Felix was a prince. And if he died, Ezinna's family would be out of power unless something magical happened, which was possible because I'd heard weirder.

CHAPTER 12

---·❋·---

BATTLE OF THE SIDEKICKS

As soon as we got to the gates, the gateman asked Felix, "What's wrong?"

Felix did not respond. I could see the looks on the guard's faces as if they wanted to hug him, but they couldn't because they were not allowed to. When we entered the palace, Felix went straight upstairs.

"I guess we have to tell Ezinna what we saw," I told Cindy.

"Yeah!" she replied.

We went to the elevator, watching Carol play with Jonah while Clair and Vincent watched TV. Then in a second, I saw Dan the lion purring at Cindy and rolling over. Cindy pressed the button, and we walked in the elevator. It didn't take time to get to the palace floor.

We bowed down and said, "Mr. Ezinna, we have news and information to tell you."

"Where is Felix!" Ezinna demanded.

"He is in his room, sir," I replied.

"Guards! Receive Felix and bring him to me immediately." The guards then ran out.

"So what is the news?" Ezinna asked.

"Uh, we saw some people in the forest at the enemy village," Cindy said. Seconds later, Felix walked in the room still looking gloomy.

"Guards! Leave! I want to be alone with these children." The guards walked out with no complaint. "What did you do to my son?"

"It's okay, Father. They didn't make me upset."

"What happened, Max?"

"We saw a huge bearded man shoot a tall slim man wearing a tie who tried to defend your honor."

"What! In Mountain of Peace?" Ezinna yelled.

"Yes, Father. I saw it too, and that's why I'm not happy."

"These people are cowards," Ezinna said.

"That means they have evolved beyond what Mountain of Peace stands for. It is unbelievable." Afterward, Cindy explained everything.

"I'll be sure to explain this in the meeting with the Council of Elders," Ezinna said. "This is certainly not good. I must see the bottom of it. I'm happy you children came. And this confirms what Chiron said to me about the research he made."

Then Felix's mother walked into the room and said, "Dinner is ready."

Pretending like nothing happened, we all rushed to the dining area, including Carol, Jonah, and Vincent, who were already seated. Ezinna stepped aside and ate in a different side arrangement while Felix mother talked with him.

After we ate dinner, we all walked to our rooms and slept. I thought about what might happen during the meeting in the morning. I thought about Magic School and what Chiron and Drake would be doing. I also thought about my mother and Grace. I thought also about the danger we might be in and if our mission was going right. Jonah was our only hope of escape if something would happen that would endanger us since he was from Mountain of Peace.

So I figured that we must make sure he was not the traitor that Ron revealed about. In a minute, my eyes rolled into sleep. I guess it was a long hard day. As I went into a deep slumber, the dreams started. I saw Zemnas sitting in his palace while I stood in front of him.

"Max, this is your destiny!" he yelled.

"No, it is not, I want to save Olympus and the world, not to control it," I replied.

Suddenly, a current of wind picked me off the ground, choking me. I saw his hand as he used his power to do it.

"Why are you doing this?" I yelled.

"Our organization is filled with one of the most powerful demigods," he said.

I used my powers to rush a powerful tsunami, but Zemnas deflected it with his powerful wind. "It is impossible to defeat me because I killed Aeolus, god of wind."

"All you are is a big stuck-up child who cried for his daddy because you did not get to love him, so you killed him."

"Aahhhhh!" he yelled.

Suddenly, I heard a voice that sounded like Cindy, and I could feel a pushing against my body. "Wake up, Max! Wake up, Max!"

Then I opened my eyes.

It was Cindy. I looked outside, and it was still kind of dark, and I said to her, "It is not yet time to get up."

"It is already five o'clock, and we must sneak out to the meeting, remember?" She said.

"Oh!" I said as I jumped up immediately.

I went ahead and brushed my teeth and was ready to go.

I said to Cindy, "How are we going to get around the guards and the gateman?"

"I have it all planned out," Cindy replied happily. "Follow my lead."

Cindy opened the door and acted as if she was sick ready to throw up.

"Oh! Oh! My stomach hurts," she said to the guards. "Max is here to help me get some fresh air outside of the compound."

The guard looked at Cindy in disbelief, but he still opened the gate.

"It feels good out here," she said, faking some kind of relief. She used her foot to close the gate.

Surprisingly, the guards did not make a move.

"You could pass for an actor," I said to Cindy while laughing.

"Be quiet, just follow," Cindy said.

"Yes, ma'am," I replied in a sarcastic way.

We walked in the same direction Felix did when he showed us the village square. When we finally got to the village square, we hid in the behind the bushes inside the hollow of a big tree to view and listen to the conversation that had already started. Nobody could see or sense us there. Then we listened to everything.

"Ezinna, the meeting requires a second in command when you go to the meeting, and I think you should take General Scar beside you because he is more experienced than everybody else," one of the elders suggested.

"Ezinna, you should be very cautious when you go to the meeting," an elder man in a red cap warned.

"I know, I know," Ezinna said frustrated. "I am here to tell you that the enemy village has become dirty cowards who use gun to fight a man's battle. We cannot just go to war with knives, bows, and spears. Who will win a fight, a skinny man with the knife or a fat man with the gun? But we cannot tolerate fat men using a gun to fight a skinny man with a knife. Nor shall we accept the killing of innocent citizens when they speak for the good of the people."

One of the elders added that the enemy village had been enemies with their village since BC, and they cannot stop the feud with kids making a peace treaty. "Therefore, it is about time grown-up men take the matter to pull the bull by the horn. Peace is the answer. Peace for now, peace forever," he concluded.

"Now let me tell you," Ezinna said. Have you heard how and why Mr. Jacob was shot in enemy village? Well, first, we all know that Mr. Jacob is an honorable man, educated and peace loving. Because he said no to a secret plot to fight my village and me, his kinsman shot and killed him in broad daylight. He was a close, dear friend, and his death would make peace a long shot from all of us. He is among the few who listens to the sound of good reasoning and peaceful ways. And we must do something about it."

"Ezinna has not told them about Chiron or us," I whispered to Cindy.

"I know, but wait," Cindy said.

"Let's go and tell them everything and that we are here to help," I said.

"No! Did you not hear them say kids would not make peace or fight for them? You just need to be still and listen to these people, then come up with our strategies when we discuss with Clair," Cindy said, frustrated.

"Okay! Okay!" I said, and I bent over, pretending as if my mind was all in the discussion. As I listened, my mind wondered about the next meeting when the bad foreigners would come, and we knew that the enemy village would be present too.

In a few minutes, the meeting ended, and Ezinna thanked all the people for their ideas. I was happy he did not say specifically that we told him anything about the secret killer.

When everybody said yeah and were about to disperse, I jumped out and shouted, "Let nobody move!" and Cindy could not help but come out too.

"Who are you?" an old man in red cap asked.

Before I could answer him, General Scar appeared from behind. "You again! What are you doing here? You heard everything, didn't you!" he yelled and then walked closer to me.

I said to him, "Step back," while I reached into my pocket for White Fang.

I sent a gust of wind to him. He spun around several times and fell down to his stomach. Then he got up, looked at me in extreme rage and daze just like all others who now were quiet. Ezinna was amazed too, and he became quiet. In my mind, I figured that Ezinna was thinking what was really happening.

I looked straight at General Scar's eyes and said, "That's what happens to people like you who have no respect for kids."

"Stop that, Max," Cindy said.

"Stop!" Ezinna said, joining with Cindy.

"Okay! With all due respect to Ezinna," I said and bowed, then I started to speak.

"Yes!" I said. "Before General Scar rudely interrupted, my name is Max, and my friend is Cindy.

We have listened and heard all the problems your village is facing. We are here to help Ezinna and his people. First, you must have General Scar stand beside Ezinna at the meeting. If the bad foreigners make trouble for you, we will come after them. Do not fear the enemy village."

"What!" one of the villagers said.

I ignored him as I made a sign to Cindy, and I said "Teleport."

Cindy threw a potion in the air and a portal appeared. We stepped in and went straight into our room in the palace and continued our sleep. This time, we did not have to mess with the guards. Jonah, Clair, Vincent, Felix, and Carol were still sleeping. We did not see Felix's mom. Maybe she was in her ranch rest house. I looked at the clock. It was 6:30 am.

A few minutes later, a big door slammed.

"Where are Max and Cindy!" Ezinna yelled.

Automatically, Felix woke and asked, "Is that my father?"

"Yeah," I said.

"What did you do to make him upset?"

"We kinda eavesdropped in the meeting," I replied. "I am scared now."

"This is the first time my dad has gotten mad in a long time," Felix added. Cindy and I went downstairs, and we saw Ezinna.

"What were you thinking sneaking into that meeting?" he said angrily.

"I'm sorry, but I wanted to know what the council would say," I replied in respect.

Then from the left side of the living room, Felix's mother entered when she heard the yelling, and she looked at us in sympathy, then turned to Ezinna, and said, "You know they are just little kids," in a very gentle voice. "Please forgive them."

Almost instantly and in a split second, he said, "Go back to your rooms and sleep."

"Come this way, Ezinna," Felix's mother said, and both of them walked away, but he turned and announced about the meeting the next day and warned that we do not show our faces. "It is a meeting of adults," he warned.

Cindy and I ran back to the room immediately. When we got in our room, Clair and Jonah had some type of map, blueprint, and diagrams.

"Oh, hi, Cindy, hi, Max," Jonah said.

"What's that?" I asked.

"Battle strategies we can use," Clair said.

I turned to Felix and asked him, "Do you know any history about your village that you would like to share with us?"

"Yeah," he replied. "It all started when our people were cavemen in BC. Our leader was Koda. His older brother, Shakka, was obsessed with power and would kill for it. Both of them were extremely gifted with intelligence and combat. Shakka and Koda were our leaders; I guess you could say that. They led our clan to victory every time they fought with other clans. One day, Shakka made a plan to scour enemy clans and take them out until they gave up and give our clan power and respect. Koda ultimately refused, and it led to one of the greatest battles in our history.

"Both were equally matched in strength. Shakka's thrive for power was no match for Koda. Shakka struck Koda on the ground. Holding his sword at the tip of Koda's throat, for some reason, he spared his brother's life.

"They then agreed to go separate ways. Half of the clan followed Shakka, and the other half followed Koda. The number of people in each group built long enough and grew to become villages. Koda called his village Mountain of Peace, and Shakka called his village Mountain of the End. That's how our villages became enemies."

As I looked at the clock hanging on the wall, I noticed it was 3:00 pm already. By that time, my jaw dropped in amazement at what had happened. Everybody else was quiet so much you could hear a pin drop in our midst.

"So the two villages were like brothers," I said, breaking the silence.

"Yes, of course," Felix acclaimed, also in disappointed mood.

I was shocked, but I enjoyed the story. I also realized that I didn't take a shower or brush my teeth yet. I rushed to the bathroom and did my hygiene. When I came out, Felix was back right in my room.

"Do you have a training ground?" I asked Felix.

"Of course," he replied.

"Where?" I added.

"Just follow me," he said.

He led me to a back door. Once he opened it, we were outside. Across from us was a super-sized dome. The dome was silver, and there was a neon sign that said Training Grounds. Felix walked to the door and knelt down.

"Why are you kneeling down?" I asked.

"For the computer to scan my eye so we can get in," he replied.

After a second, the electronic door opened. Inside the dome was a wooden gym filled with punching bags and target posts.

"So what do you want to do, Max?" Felix asked. "Build up my speed and endurance."

"Then I have just a right section for you," he replied happily.

The dome was split into five equal parts, each representing a stat. The first one was strength, second was speed, third was intelligence, fourth was endurance, and fifth was balance.

"I think we should go to the speed section then go to the endurance section," Felix suggested.

"Why can't I just go to all of them?" I asked.

"Because you would pass out, plus it's impossible," he replied.

I walked to the speed section, and there was a huge entrance along with the other sections. When we halfway entered the section, there was a front desk with a lady behind it.

"How are you today, Felix?" the lady said.

"Oh! Good," he replied.

"So who's the new guy?" she asked again.

"My friend."

"What shall the training course be?"

"The usual," Felix replied.

Suddenly, the automatic sliding door behind her opened, and she said, "Have a happy training." As we entered the room, I noticed Felix was smiling.

"This is it," Felix said happily.

After a few seconds, a big black iron ball came hurling at me. I jumped out the way, and I yelled, "What was that!"

"It's the training course," Felix said, laughing. The iron ball was chained to the ceiling. The iron ball came back and forth, and I kept dodging it. I had a brilliant but stupid plan, and I did it. When it came toward me again, I jumped on top of the ball. I used White Fang to slash the chain that held the iron ball to swing back and forth. Suddenly, the ball fell hard.

"Nice, but can you handle this?" Felix said. Then I looked to the left and saw a fat man with two large sticks. He ran faster than I thought. Every time he chased me, I ran. Felix kept telling me to stop. When I finally stopped, he got his two big sticks and started to hit my feet with them. I lifted my feet up and down to dodge and my strategy worked. When he became tired, I slashed him in half with my sword. Luckily, it was a robot. I started panting and told Felix that I was tired.

"Whatever, let's go to the strength section," he replied.

As tired as I was, I agreed. We walked out of the section, and there was a different lady standing at the front table. We walked over to the strength section, and the desk lady set everything up for us. As we walked in the room, there was a cage in front of us. Between the cages, I could see a huge animal hybrid. On the right was a ring of weapons.

Felix ran to it and asked me whether I wanted anything.

"I'll stick with my sword," I replied.

Felix grabbed a spear with a special curved metal tip.

"What are you doing with that?" I asked.

"I'm fighting with you," he replied.

I turned forward and opened the cage. The beast roared.

Felix ran with immense speed and attacked the monster in the head. The creature had brown tentacles, huge hands, and sharp teeth. The monster used its tentacle to grab Felix. I ran toward him and jumped on the monster. I used White Fang to slash the tentacle, and Felix fell down.

"Thanks!" he yelled at me while he attacked the creature again. He used his spear to stab the monster in the eye. I could hear a large roar after. Felix single-handedly killed the monster. Every time it used its tentacle to hit Felix, Felix remembered the training in the speed section and used my strategy to dodge.

I never realized how strong Felix was even if he wasn't a demigod. After Felix killed the monster, it blew up cybernetically.

"I think we should be getting back to the palace," Felix suggested.

"I know," I replied.

We walked out of the dome and headed for the palace. We were back outside and we saw the back door. When we were finally in the palace, I looked at the time, and it was already 6:00. I turned, and Felix was gone.

I went to my room; Clair and Vincent were still working on battle strategies and tactics. "You guys are still working on that?" I asked.

"Yeah, we need to finish this before tomorrow," Clair replied. Suddenly, I fell on the ground in tiredness.

I woke up the next morning, brushed my teeth, and got ready for the big meeting. Cindy and Jonah were waiting for me, and I was ready.

"Where are they having this meeting anyway?" I asked confused.

"We are taking a special portal that can take us somewhere that we haven't been yet," Cindy stated. Jonah threw the potion, and we appeared behind some boxes at the meeting. It looked like the place was at the top of a building.

In front of us was a big table with the foreigners. One of them was old, and his representative had a bulletproof vest. The enemy village had the same fat man who killed that other man, and his representative was wearing a black suit. And there was Ezinna. His representative was General Scar.

First, I knew the foreigner's name was Eugene and the representative's was Germane. The fat man's name was Bruce and his representative's was Mark. They were discussing and arguing about why Ezinna should give up his estate. I noticed that the foreigners and the enemy village were ganging up on Ezinna about giving up his lands and his village estate.

As soon as Ezinna yelled no, Germane pulled out a handgun and tried to shoot Ezinna, but General Scar acted quickly and used his spear to deflect the bullet toward the glass above us, and it shattered. General Scar ran toward Germane and struck. Mark also pulled a gun out and shot. For every single bullet they shot, General Scar either cut it in half or deflected it. Mark tackled General Scar into the large glass window in front of the meeting table. They were falling down into the bottom. Amazingly, Germane flew out to the ground.

"You see what happens when you don't cooperate," Eugene said to Ezinna, chuckling.

I saw the facial expression on Bruce's face as he shifted uneasily. I jumped from the corner and uncapped White Fang.

I pointed it at Eugene and said, "how dare you threaten Ezinna."

"What is a kid doing pointing a sword at me?" he said. "Hasn't your mother told you not to play with sharp objects?"

I had a feeling both of them weren't armed, so I told Cindy to look after them while I helped General Scar.

I jumped out from the window, and it was a very far jump, as from the Empire State Building. Hopefully, there was a couch to cushion my landing. But there wasn't. I fell on top of Mark. Germane pointed his gun at me, but General Scar slapped the gun out of his hand. I used my sword and slashed Germane in the chest. General Scar then picked Germane up and threw him.

"Thanks, kid," he said to me. "I guess you kind of helped, little boy."

"Shut up!" I replied. "Concentrate on your job before they cut off your neck."

Then Jonah, Felix, and Clair rushed in from the sky in a

portal, and we took control to defeat the bad foreigners and the enemy village. They were rounded up.

"What shall we do with these people?" General Scar asked Ezinna.

"In the meantime, receive the guards here immediately," he said.

General Scar made a sound and about one thousand guards appeared. "The guards are here," General Scar said to Ezinna.

"Good! Guards, you know what to do. Take them to jail until I meet with the Council of Elders.

They are not to see the sky in jail until the council meets in ninety days."

"What about the non-conflict agreement," Cindy interrupted. "We are here to stop all the feuds and fighting."

"Ezinna, do you have an attorney in your council or in this village," I asked.

"No," Ezinna announced.

"Then we need to speak with Chiron," I said.

I brought out the mirror to knock on it and connect to him. I tapped it as usual, but there was no immediate response, and then Drake came on.

"Drake, is that you? I need to speak with Chiron now."

"Hold on, it is Max," he said, and Chiron came. "Max, what is it, is Ezinna doing okay?"

"Yes, sir," I said in a proud voice.

"So what do you want, and how is the mission?" he asked.

"Mission is good, but we have a problem. First, we are able to round up the leaders of the bad foreigners and the enemy village who wanted to kill Ezinna to take his lands and village estate. They are here, looking at us, and Ezinna is here too. Second, Ezinna has ordered that they be jailed. Third, we are suggesting that we get them to sign an agreement never to fight or plan something bad against Ezinna, but there is no lawyer. We need you to teleport the agreement to Cindy's laptop."

"Good job," he said. "Consider it done. It was already sent to Cindy's laptop. Ask her to print it out copies for each of you,

Ezinna, the bad foreigners, the enemy village, Cindy, Vincent, Clair, Jonah, and I. Can I speak with Ezinna?"

"Sure." And I handed it over to Ezinna.

"Ezinna, it's me, Chiron. How are Max and the other kids doing there?"

"They are wonderful," he replied.

"Okay! Good! Work with them because they are there to help."

"All right, my good friend," Ezinna said.

"Let me speak with Max," Chiron said.

At this time, I became worried and nervous because Chiron started another mission by always coming with words to make me regret ever thinking of abandoning the mission with "drastic times call for drastic measures." And I am not ready to hear that, I thought in my mind.

"Yes, sir," I said.

"You and your friends have done a good job, and report to Magic School once you have completely finished."

I put the mirror back in my pocket while everybody moped.

Then I turned to Cindy and Clair and asked, "What are you doing looking at me like that?"

"The agreements are ready," they said and handed me the printout in long sheets of paper correctly with the names of the parties.

"Now everybody, listen," I said screaming. "I am about to read the armistice for the sad development in this clan. I'm gonna read the following document as hereby written.

Pledge by Mountain of the End and Bad Foreigners Not to Fight or Gang Against Ezinna, His Estate, and His Village of Mountain of Peace.

"It reads,

Be it known by all men, living and dead, mortals, gods, Titan lords, and demigods that from this date forward we, the people of Mountain of the End and the bad foreigners, have ceased and have desisted and would no longer fight directly or indirectly, gang up against Ezinna, his Estate, and his village of Mountain of Peace.

If there become disagreements on any matter, henceforth, such would be discussed, mutually negotiated, and settled without gunfire or other acts of war, gang up, or fight.

We also pledge never to mess with Max, Cindy, Clair, Jonah, and Vincent or their master for defeating us, and we hereby agree to any punishment they, Ezinna and the Council of Elders, will give us.

Signed this June 15, 2010, at Mountain of Peace, Nigeria, West Africa. By and on behalf of all the people and ourselves, we represent.

X Germane & Eugene

Germane and Eugene/The bad foreigners) X Bruce & Mark

Witnessed by: Bruce and Mark/Mountain of the End X Felix, Vincent, Jonah, Cindy, & Max

Felix, Cindy, Vincent, Jonah, and Max/For the kids) X Ezinna & General Scar

Accepted by: Ezinna and General Scar/Mountain of Peace

"Does anybody object?" I asked when I finished reading.

They all said, "No!"

"It is a deal," I said.

"Sign here," I said as they put marks beside the X. Then Cindy and I signed. That sealed the deal, and I gave every party a copy.

That is how we arranged the agreement for peace, and we asked Ezinna to force the bad foreigners to leave immediately after ninety days without achieving their goal. That is how Ezinna was finally helped to make peace between Mountain of Peace and Mountain of the End. After all, kids made the peace treaty and had an armistice that stuck without bloodshed.

But the only thing in my mind was, would the peace stay forever? Nobody knows, I answered to myself.

Then I had an idea. I needed to speak with Ezinna about Felix so that he wouldn't get harmed.

CHAPTER 13

✳

BOOS AND JOYS

Felix and I, for some reason, had bonded. After everybody signed the contract, we teleported back to the palace.

Ezinna was already there, and I asked Ezinna whether it was okay for Felix to go to America with us so nothing will happen to him, so he can retain the title as king when he becomes older.

"You know, this will save Felix in case the war breaks out again so that he doesn't get killed preserving power to your heir and family." I tried to press the point for my new friend, Felix.

"I'll think about it," Ezinna replied. "But in the meantime, let's celebrate our victory. Tonight we're going to have a ceremony, and I've already informed the guards to tell the villagers to gather, decorate, and plan."

Then I thought about Chiron, if he would take Felix to live in and attend Magic School too. So I went back to Ezinna to ask his permission.

For some reason, the others finally teleported back after our conversation.

"Sorry for the wait, we stopped and got ice cream on the way," Vincent said while he licked his chocolate ice cream.

Felix quickly finished his and ran upstairs to his room.

A minute later, he came back with a first aid kit and said to me, "Lift your pants up."

"What are you doing?" I asked him.

"I know you're injured, so I decided to use my medical training skills and heal it."

I was injured, but I tried to shake it off. I lifted my pants up and smiled. He first sprayed alcohol and wiped it with a germ-killing tissue. Then he picked out the dead skin, and he wrapped it around with a bandage.

"Wow," I said while pulling my pant leg down. Felix ran back to his room happily.

"That's my son," Ezinna said.

"I already know that," I said, thinking that he was talking to me.

Then he continued, "My son has been training really hard in different subjects to become a better king than me, and when he met you, you inspired him to train harder." Felix came down again, and Ezinna started to speak.

"Felix, you have spent nine years here in Mountain of Peace and have served all your working rites. The only thing left is for you to get a better education," Ezinna said. "You will go to America, in New York City with Max and his friends and get your education there and come back for college."

"Yes!" Felix yelled as he jumped up.

I smiled a little too, pretending not to be excited.

Carol wanted to go, but I wondered what my mom would say because I did not tell her about Felix yet. It would be hard, but with Carol, it would be harder, I thought.

I felt bad when I saw tears roll down her cheeks.

I went close and said, "I know. It's okay. We will be back." Then she brightened up and wiped out her tears.

"The festival doesn't start until an hour, so you all are free to do anything," Ezinna said. Everybody ran upstairs and freshened up. Too bad we didn't own suits to wear, but we managed. Cindy even washed Dan. In an hour, we all were ready.

We walked to the village square, and it was full and many

people were there. There were blue, white, red, and green-lit candles inside little see-through globes. A nice try that showed off the colors of American and Nigerian flags.

A microphone stood on top of the stage, foods wrapped and covered in aluminum foils as well as different drinks were there too.

The DJ played different music and tunes.

After everybody ate and danced a little, it was time for awards.

First up was General Scar. It was the first time I had seen General Scar and Ezinna in a suit. At the microphone was Ezinna saying General Scar's award. "I would like to thank General Scar for his long-term services in my security section. He has battled through the hard times when his parents weren't there and has shown loyalty and focus when fighting for his village. He has not thought of revenge against the murderers of his family so that's why he has earned the right for his rank to be boosted up to Top Chief Security and Black Ops," Ezinna said while he held up a gold trophy to General Scar.

General Scar came up to the microphone and took the trophy from Ezinna and held it up higher while crying. After General Scar said his long sob speech, it was me and my friend's turn to receive an award.

"Next, I would like to congratulate Cindy, Clair, Jonah, Vincent, and Max," Ezinna said happily. My friends and I walked on stage behind Ezinna.

Then Ezinna continued, "I would like to present this award because they have been extremely helpful to this village. No matter what the challenge, they still found a way to make peace. Even though I told them to stay home and that it was too dangerous, they cared about my well being enough to risk their lives and help me, so this is why I'm giving them this award." Everybody started to clap amazingly. Ezinna then gave us all gold trophies and shook our hands. Then he said, "I also give you full access to use part of my estate as both a staging place and training in the future."

This was an area designated for grazing, and it was like my

school times ten, I imagined.

When I looked to the left, I saw the bad foreigners and the enemy village. When we got off stage, Ezinna announced something.

"Foreigners here, instead of punishing you, I will send you to Siberia, then from there, you can go to wherever you came from. You are never to come to Mountain of Peace or any place in Nigeria. You will be stripped of all your weapons or instruments except your passports and clothes. You must be escorted with a private helicopter to the nearest international airport by a pilot and eight guards. Thank you, and you may now proceed to the helicopter there." The black helicopter landed in front of the village square. As they boarded the helicopter, the villagers booed them.

"Enemy village representatives, we have seen your regret and have offered you another opportunity. To make peace with us and live together, I hereby give you amnesty from Mountain of Peace, but you must report to your headman and serve for ninety days before being released. So do you accept?"

"Yes, sir!" They replied.

"General Scar, escort them to Mountain of the End, also escort Max and friends back to the palace."

When we were back at the palace, everybody fell to the couch and slept because tomorrow was going to be a big day. I woke up watching my friends getting ready. I got up and packed my clothes.

Once we were all ready, I asked Cindy how we were going to get back to New York.

She said, "Ezinna will lend us a private jet able to fit ten people with comfortable seats, TV, and two bathrooms."

"Why can't we just use a portal or a potion to get us there?"

"Because a potion won't let us travel that far and a portal is too complicated to summon at this time," she replied.

"Huh!" I huffed to myself.

Once everybody was fully ready, Felix's mother came out along with Ezinna and Carol. They said good-bye.

The private jet was gray.

"Who's going to fly it?" I asked Ezinna.

"It is set on autopilot, and the course is set to Magic School, New York, so you all are good to go."

We thanked Ezinna for his care and kindness toward us. We thanked him for the people of Mountain of Peace, and we promised to be back when the need comes.

"Watch out and be careful!" Ezinna yelled as the jet took off. And we waved back as they waved good-bye. And I noticed that Carol was sobbing.

CHAPTER 14

A GOD ALMOST ROASTS ME ALIVE

As we got into steady altitude, I started thinking about my mom and how she's doing. I also thought about if Magic School had changed. Then I began to think about how Mountain of Peace would get along with the enemy village. I closed my eyes for one second, and I was sleepy. Unfortunately, it was another nightmare. I saw Felix in Mountain of Peace. It was thundering and raining. Felix was grown- up and was standing on top of a rock. In front of him were villagers in shackles, bowing down to him.

Behind him in the shadows was a male figure but was hard to see his face. You could also notice that Mountain of Peace and Mountain of the End were combined as one, making that area large. I could tell Felix was under the influence of the man in the shadow. I tried to think of a way to prevent this future because I knew Felix was better than this. Felix didn't come all this way just to become evil, I thought in my mind.

Then I heard a rumbling sound that could've been coming from the engine. Suddenly, I woke up and everybody started panicking.

"What happened?" I asked.

"The plane ran out of fuel!" Vincent replied.

"What!" I yelled.

Then we started arguing what to do. I saw Felix sneak to the steering wheel. "What are you doing!" I yelled at him.

"There is just enough fuel to land this thing," Felix replied. "I am going to alter the autopilot to land now."

He pulled the steering wheel back, made some adjustments on the dashboard, and started to glide the plane, first by shutting down the fuel supply. And he cut all the engines off, and he manipulated it to hold it steady.

I looked at the location map, and there was a nearby fishing dock. But all I was worried about was how softly we were going to land it. As we were gliding, I could feel the amplitude of the air. All of us standing fell and started sliding up and down on the floor . . . When we were close to the dock, Felix made the plane straight to land it. When it was on the actual dock, it rolled to the tip of it. Barely making it, he avoided a catastrophe.

Then we could hear loud attacking sounds. I looked out the jet's window and saw Xemas and Ares fighting. I went to Cindy, and I whispered in her ear. "Cindy, what do we do? Black Hand is here fighting Ares."

"We help Ares defeat him," she replied.

Cindy and I ran outside and our friends followed. Ares looked like a biker. He had black hair with an army haircut. He had on a biker jacket with a dark purple inner shirt and had on black jeans. His motorcycle wasn't far away from him. His motorcycle was black with flames coming from it. Ares had a long scar on the side of his cheek, but his eyes were like ongoing fire.

Suddenly, Ares shot fireballs out his eyes at Xemas, but he dodged, and it reached me. Luckily, it didn't hit me directly, but it singed my shirt. I summoned a tsunami wave, but somehow, Xemas created a black hole, and it swallowed the water up.

"Max, you betrayed us, so I'm going to kill you and Ares!" he yelled.

"Traitor!" Ares yelled at me. "I knew the sea boy's son couldn't be trusted."

Ares summoned a spiked club. He tried to hit Xemas, but he dodged again. Ares quickly substituted his club for a sword.

"How can Ares change his weapon?" I asked Cindy.

"Because that's one of his powers," she replied.

Ares unleashed flames of fire while Xemas did the same thing, but Xemas's fire was black. When the two flames met, they were evenly matched, but after a few seconds, Xemas's fire overcame Ares's. Afterward, Ares landed on the ground. Due to the flame, he substituted his sword for a black guitar with fire designs. Ares floated in the air and unleashed a series of intense sound waves. It was so loud when we covered our ears; we still heard the intensity of it. It made Xemas fly all the way in the area where the water was. Then for some reason, Xemas broke into a berserk state. Dark winds started to flow recklessly, and Xemas's eyes went blank light yellow. His scar that was shaped like an X grew slightly bigger.

"Arrrrh!" Xemas yelled.

He jumped in the air and started to fly. Then he sent dark lightning, and it struck Ares. Jonah stored his energy and meditated. When Xemas saw Jonah open for an attack, he flew to attack. As soon as he was close, Jonah unfolded a large amount of fire.

"Uhhh!" Xemas yelled in pain.

Luckily, he was burned on the chest. Xemas gasped for breath, and Ares had a chance to kill him. Ares substituted his guitar for a spiked wheel attached to a long free chain. Ares then swung it with intense speed. It struck Xemas in the back instantly. Surprisingly, he didn't die. He gasped for breath again. Xemas then summoned a claymore to his hand. It was huge. Most of it was light blue with a yellow grip. The sword part wasn't like a normal sword. First, it's skinny, then it's a fat part with six spikes. Xemas removed the weapon out of his back and got up.

He flew with intense speed and attempted to hit Ares but missed. Then there was a rumbling in the ground. Suddenly, a big black hand with an eerie chill erupted from the floor. It grabbed Ares to the floor, and Xemas lowered to where Ares was. He hit him in the face a few times and said, "You're dead." Xemas dropped his weapon and put his hands on Ares' chest. Then unleashed immensely charged black electricity.

"Arghhhhhhhhh!" Ares yelled.

I uncapped White Fang and ran to Xemas. Jonah and Vincent followed. Cindy, Clair, and Felix stood by, confused about what was happening. This was the first time he had seen an encounter outside Mountain of Peace. As we ran, the only one without a weapon was Vincent. But he looked at the ground and started walking. He picked up a stick and bendable grass weeds. He tied them together with some rubber bands in his pocket and made a bow. He picked up more sticks and tied it with a sharp rock. As soon as he did that, he shot the handmade arrow. Xemas used his hand and caught it at the tip.

"Now I'm going to get serious with you kids," Xemas said angrily.

Jonah got his spear and conducted electricity. Jonah and I struck at the same time, but Xemas countered it. He used his claymore and started swinging. I dodged a couple of times, but he hit me a couple of the other times. When Jonah tried to strike him from behind Xemas defended himself with his claymore.

"Hey! Kid, might wanna help me outta here?" Ares asked Vincent.

Vincent struggled to free him from the huge hand. When Ares was freed, he summoned his sword and sliced the hand in half. When he was free, he unleashed a wave of heat. It was really hot, and even Xemas was worn out. I had my chance, but Ares cut me off purposely and summoned a barbwire bat. He bashed it on his head and picked him by the neck with one hand.

"Listen here, pal! Who do you think you are comin' my way, tryin' to start fights!" Ares yelled. Once Ares threw him into the sand, Xemas mumbled, "I'd get you next time," while he teleported. Ares walked toward me and said, "This doesn't change anything, seaweed boy."

He grabbed his barbwire bat and swung at me, but quickly, I dodged.

"I just helped you, and you're still trying to kill me!" I cried.

"You betrayed everyone, you rotten stink!" He replied aggressively.

I created an earthquake, but it didn't seem to affect him. He summoned a morning star and swung it at me. It scratched the surface of my skin but still missed. It was time to stop being a baby; I was finally going to fight back. When he swung both of them, I cut off the chain of the morning star and struck his chest. He touched my sword, and it heated up. It was so hot it reached to the handle of the sword. I dropped my sword before getting burned. He touched the ground with both hands, and the whole beach ground got burning hot. I jumped up and down, trying not to feel the heat. I picked up my sword, hoping it wasn't still hot. I slashed him then he started to bleed gold. Suddenly, it healed.

"You can't kill a god that easily," he said.

"Why do you hate me?" I asked.

He replied, "Because you betrayed Olympus and me."

He unleashed a series of flames at me. Half my clothes were burned, and I coughed up some ash.

Jonah stepped in front of me and started to talk to Ares. "He isn't a bad kid, and he isn't a traitor."

He grinned at me and said, "I'll let it slide this time, but next time you try something like this, I'll really roast you alive." Then he teleported in flames.

CHAPTER 15

———— ❋ ————

I POP MY FUNNY BONE

❝How are we going to get to Magic School and return this plane," I asked.

"Well, there are sea gas tanks here that can also fuel planes, ships, and cars," Jonah replied.

"Then what are we doing just standing here?" Vincent said.

We all ran to the supply room and grabbed a numerous number of tanks. Then we ran back and forth to the plane and filled the gas up. After everybody boarded the jet, Felix set it to autopilot on its original destination, Magic School.

Once the jet took off, I couldn't wait to be back. I didn't know what I was going to do first, but I didn't care.

The trip to Magic School wasn't far; it only took ten minutes. It was somehow morning. Then we landed in the parking lot in front of the Music Studio. The New York's Hottest Jam's neon sign was kind of dim with the A in "Jams" missing. Vincent walked to the door and opened it. When we were in the studio, it looked the same as before—junky and messy.

"I thought we're going to Magic School," Felix cried.

"I said the same thing too when it was my first time." I unlocked the entrance, and we were in Magic School.

"I'm still not seeing anything!" Felix yelled.

"Oh, I forgot!" Cindy yelled at herself.

"What?" I asked.

"I forgot Felix is still a mortal, and the magic boundary doesn't enable him to see anything magical."

"Luckily, I carried a magical vision herb," Vincent said happily.

The herb was green dust within a sandwich bag. Vincent took a handful of it and threw it in Felix's eye.

After three seconds, Felix said, "Wow! This is Magic School?"

"Yeah, great isn't it?" I said.

When I turned, Clair was gone and Vincent was leaving.

"Where are you going?" I asked.

"To get back to my office and finish my work," Vincent replied.

"But we just got back," I said.

"Yeah, I've missed a lot of my deadlines, and I have to catch up with them," he replied, and he left.

"So what are you guys gonna do?" I asked the rest.

"I might meditate," Jonah said.

"I'll go meet up with Chiron," Cindy added.

"Felix and I will come with you," I said.

"Sure," she replied.

As we walked, we bumped into a tall figure. When I looked up, it was Chiron.

"Master Chiron! What's up," I said happily

"Max, how are you?" he replied. "So you have already finished the mission."

"Yeah, finally," I said.

He looked at Felix in astonishment. "So you're Felix, the prince I've been hearing about. It's nice to see you in person," he said.

Felix chuckled.

"So, Chiron, should I leave him with you?" I asked.

"Yeah, you go to your dorm and see the classes you take," he replied.

I tried to remember where my dorm was then I started to walk. Fortunately, I saw it. When I entered the room, I saw Lucas and Cindy, flirting as usual. Lucas looked at me and smiled.

"So I guess you have the same classes with Cindy and me," he said.

I grinned tightly and turned to the class schedule. Cindy was only in two of my classes. Lucas was in all of mine. My body instantly flew with anger.

"When does class start?" I asked Cindy.

"Now," Lucas replied.

"I didn't ask you," I said fiercely.

"Class really does start now," Cindy added.

I looked at the schedule again, and swords practice was the first class. I walked around Magic School looking for the room, and I found it. As soon as I was in front of the door, it opened. I saw Drake leading a long line of kids my age.

"You're late for class, Max," Drake said.

"Sorry, just came back from a mission."

Lucas and Cindy came running down the hallway, laughing.

"Lucas, you have no excuse for being late, so I'm gonna have to account you absent," Drake announced.

Lucas groaned, and Drake told us all to get to the back of the line. We walked all the way to the gym, and it was filled with fighting equipment.

Then Drake announced that today we'll be training in the gym. "Everybody, pick a partner," he said.

When I was about to pick Cindy, Lucas ran to me. "We'll be partners," Lucas said sinisterly.

"Everybody, take out your swords and duel," Drake instructed.

I uncapped White Fang, and Lucas pulled out his sword.

"I call my sword Star Killer," Lucas said. "You jealous of me? Why not just attack me." He taunted me until I was tired of it. I slashed with incredible strength.

"I thought you would be a good sword fighter, like your brother, but it looks like it skipped a generation," Lucas yelled.

"Arrgh!" I grunted.

He nearly dodged all my blows. In the matter of two minutes, everybody surrounded us and watched. Every time I struck, he dodged. I think it was due to the fact that he was the son of Hermes. When he attacked, he hit me with intense speed. When he was about to use his super speed to run again, I made a huge earthquake.

My earthquakes increase when I'm mad. The earthquake was so strong, it shook him out of balance, and he fell face-first. He got up quick and aimed for my shoulder.

Suddenly, my body had a quick reaction because General Scar injured me there before. I was paralyzed there, but I could still fight. When I held my arm in pain, he quickly clotheslined me. The impact of my fall was crazy. My back felt like I slept in a pile of thumbtacks. He pointed his sword at my neck. I used my other hand with the sword to swipe his sword away, and it took me a while to get up. Our swords clashed aimlessly for minutes.

Then I remembered what Drake taught me before the mission. As soon as Lucas slashed, I countered fast but not as fast as I expected. I countered it, and he was open for a blow. When I was going to hit him in the leg, my shoulder started to hurt again. I tried to shake off the pain, then I attacked him in the leg. He fell on his knees.

"Who's crying now!" I yelled.

I summoned the Blade of Pandora in my other hand, and it started to glow black. When it was ready to fire, I withdrew both of my swords, remembering that I was good, and even though I hated Lucas, I couldn't kill him. I held my hand out and helped him up.

"I was just playing," Lucas said.

Then I could hear clapping. It was coming from Drake. "You both put together strong combos that were mixed with sword fighting and powers," Drake said amazingly. "Class dismissed."

My next class was archery, but my shoulder was killing me. I went straight to the infirmary. I walked in the nurse's office, and I saw an old lady.

She looked at me and said, "What's the matter, sweetie?"

"My shoulder," I replied.

She did an x-ray and said that I popped my elbow, and it should feel tingly and weird, but kids like to call it the funny bone. She also said that it would heal in a few hours.

I left and went to archery class. In archery class, Vincent was teaching. I still couldn't know why an eleven-year-old was a teacher.

After archery, I went to Chiron's office, and I asked Felix what to do with the jet. "What jet?" Chiron asked.

"Oh, we used a jet that Ezinna gave us. Sorry I didn't tell you."

Felix turned and stood up. Once we went outside, Felix went inside the jet and pressed some buttons.

"What did you do?" I asked.

"I set the jet on reverse autopilot so it can go to Mountain of Peace exactly where it came from," he replied.

He put it on go, and the jet took off. We walked back to Magic School, and we both went separate directions.

CHAPTER 16

❁

I BECOME A SCARED BABY

After all the classes I took, the obvious thing I did next was go to sleep. It took a while for me to sleep, and when I finally did, I had the worst nightmare. It was the same, the dream I had before about Felix. This time, they were in Ezinna's palace. Felix was alone with the man in the high chairs. Felix looked more evil than he did before. The other man's face was still covered by the shadows. They were talking about world domination.

"How are we going to dominate the world if I don't even have the power to do so?" Felix asked. After the discussion was finished, Felix got out of the chair and stood. Then the scenery changed.

They were at the top of Mountain of Peace. Everybody was working hard in a nearby field. They didn't even have decent tools. When one man asked for a break, Felix had a baritone voice. And it got really deep and he yelled, "No! Shut up!"

Suddenly, two giant gravel hands came out of the ground and nearly squished the man to death. "Do you still want a break?" Felix continued.

"No, sir," the man replied, scared.

The man in the shadows laughed greatly, and by the looks of

things, the man in the shadows was using Felix.

Once the shadows covering the man's face were gone, I saw an old man whose face was partially torn up. Then I saw a girl that may be thirteen crawling from the corner of a wall. She looked raggedy. Her clothes were tattered, and she had wounds all over her body.

"Felix," the girl said tiredly as if she had lifted the sky up. Then the girl looked familiar. She was Carol.

"Please stop this madness," she continued.

"No! Who are you?" he replied, mad as ever.

"You have a problem," she said. "And it's because of that man why you are like this."

Suddenly, the scenery changed. I could tell it was in the past because of peace. The sky wasn't dark or thundering. Everywhere wasn't combined. Then I saw Ezinna walking down the street. He was walking with Felix. Felix was somewhat older.

All of a sudden, there was a big thump. They ran quickly from where they heard the noise. They looked farther, and there was an old man. It was the same man from the future who might have turned Felix into evil. The man was unconscious. They took him to a medical building. When the man was fully healed, Ezinna asked a lot of questions.

"Why did you get unconscious? And where did you come from," he asked again.

"I . . . really don't know," he replied.

"Well, how about you become a villager in this village?" Ezinna offered.

"That would be great," he said happily. He looked at Felix and asked, "Is this your son?"

"Yes, he will be king one day."

The man looked at Felix again and smiled cruelly.

"By the way, I didn't catch your name," Ezinna said as he left.

"Ahab," he replied.

Ezinna squinted his eyes in shock.

When they left the room, Ahab put some kind of powder in a drink beside him. Five minutes later, Ezinna and Felix had ice packs in their hands. They set it on the man's head. Ezinna took the drink beside the man and drank.

He took the drink out of his mouth and said, "My drink tastes funny."

Then he collapsed. Felix looked at his father for a second and started to cry. "Nurse!" Felix yelled.

"What happened?" Ahab said.

"My father, he's—," suddenly, he paused when the nurse came.

When they put Ezinna in a bed beside Ahab, they found what had happened to him. They claimed his heart strained itself because of stress.

"He needs to recover, but he'll survive," the nurse stated.

Felix washed his tears up and went to his father's bed. Two days passed, Ahab and Ezinna were okay. Ahab fit in with the village perfectly. Everybody liked him, including Felix. But Felix liked Ahab too much. He basically hanged around him every minute of the day as if they were father and son.

Then one sad day, Ezinna had a meeting with the Council of Elders and had a sudden heart attack. Ezinna would've survived if the medics had come faster. Felix and Carol had a nervous breakdown at the funeral. Ahab was there, but he wasn't sympathetic. His heart felt nothing for a man who allowed him in as his own.

A month passed by, and Ahab was talking to Felix. "I killed your father," he said in suspense.

"You monster!" Felix yelled.

He held his fist almost hitting Ahab, but Ahab lowered the fist and said, "It was better for you."

"Why?" Felix asked as tears unleashed from his eyes.

"He held you back from accomplishing your true power. You don't realize how strong you are," Ahab told Felix.

Suddenly, the dream ended.

I woke up scared of my own shadow. I got up from my bed and went out the room. It was about ten something. It was casually dark, then I saw Felix walking with Chiron. Felix's shadow was large, just like the evil older self of him in the dream. I somewhat flinched in fear

"Hello, Max! What are you doing up?" Chiron asked.

"Uh! I've been sleeping since like six o'clock," I replied.

"Felix, you know where your room is, right?" Chiron said.

"Yeah! Goodnight, Master Chiron," Felix said before he left.

"Chiron, can I speak to you in your office," I said.

"Sure," he replied, confused.

When we got in his office, he asked, "What is the problem?"

"I've been having dreams, dreams about bad stuff."

"What was your latest dream?"

"Felix becoming a complete warlord who was then emotionless and only cared about himself. He was the complete opposite of himself."

"Well, I have a rash explanation for those dreams."

"What?" I yelled. "It drives me crazy."

"They are called premonitions," he explained.

"I know that, but what causes it?"

Chiron then lectured. "Premonitions are a gift. It is a privilege that can determine the future. People who have mastered it can have one without sleeping, and can also make themselves have one."

"But it is the dream of a bad future, who would want to have a premonition about something bad?"

"Exactly, most premonitions can be prevented. But only good people would want to prevent things that are bad. Max, embrace your power," Chiron added.

"My powers are deadly, but okay," I replied.

"Anything else you want to discuss about?" he said happily.

"What school will Felix be going to?"

"Melody Creek for Higher Learning Boarding School."

"Why can't he stay here at Magic School?"

"Because he's not a half blood, plus he doesn't even have the spark to see magical things. Max, do you know what month it is?"

"Uh, July," I said.

"No, August, it is almost time for you to go back to school, and your mother is coming to pick you up tomorrow, so in the morning, put your stuff together."

"What about the traitor?" I asked angrily.

"Maybe we could catch the traitor next summer, but for now, I'm going to make a speech about the incident. Go get some sleep Max," he said worriedly.

Once I left the room, I heard some noises in the gym. Instead of going to Chiron, I went straight to the gym. When I got there, the door was unlocked. But I realized that someone had rigged the door open with force. When I opened it, the door was nearly torn apart. The lights were out, and I still heard the noise.

I walked to the noise and something shook me and said, "Boo!" I turned, and it was Lucas.

"What are you doing in here?" I whispered.

"Magic School is almost over, and I want to find the traitor before all of us leave."

"But why are you doing it by yourself?"

"I'm not. I have an accomplice."

"Who is that?"

"Cindy," he replied.

"What are you going to do once you find the traitor?"

"Get my reward and get the prize money."

I shook my head in shame. "So where is Cindy?"

"Looking for clues," he replied.

"Max! What are you doing here?" Cindy asked with burglar clothes on.

"Lucas told me all about your plan," I said.

"Well, go back to your room before you get us caught," she whispered.

"Sure," I said sarcastically.

I went back to bed like everybody said I should. Before you knew it, I was already asleep. But I knew before I was ready to go back home I might have another nightmare.

And I was right. I was in the underworld, and it was darker and colder than usual. Most of it was crumbled and dusty. Hades was fighting a huge volcanic-like figure that was the same height as him. The man had a mini volcano sticking out of his back. His whole body was like rocks and lava. He had no hair but a nose, and his eyes were made out of fire and looked like he could take on five gods at once.

"Why are you doing this, Atlas?" Hades asked.

"It's part of Kronos's invasion to destroy Olympus and all the gods, and you could join us and rule wherever you like than this wretched, filthy place you call the underworld," he replied.

"As much as I would like to join you, I like Olympus, but the gods, I don't like so much," Hades said.

"Good, then join us."

"Eh, I don't think so, you Titans lost the war the first time, and you'll lose again."

"Fine by me, but when you're trembling at the Titans' feet, don't say I didn't warn you."

"Whatever!" Hades yelled.

Hades sent a whole bunch of dead skeletons with weapons after Atlas.

Then I tried to remember who Atlas was. Then it came to me. Atlas was punished to hold the earth and the heavens on his back for all eternity, but I wondered if he was not holding it up now, who is?

Atlas zoomed fire out of his hands. Hades nearly dodged it, then I woke up. I could see the daylight shining in my face.

CHAPTER 17

DRAG BACK TO SCHOOL

I woke up and got ready quickly. I took a quick shower and brushed my teeth. I packed all my stuff, and I was ready to go. I went out of my room and looked back, and Cindy wasn't in her bed. When I was out in the main hall, I heard Chiron yelling. I went to his office and saw Cindy and Lucas in the two chairs in front of his desk.

"Do you know how much trouble you're going to be in!" Chiron yelled. "Breaking entrances, sneaking into unauthorized places," he said, listing the things they did. "It's not good to eavesdrop, Max!"

I came out from the corner I was hiding in and said, "How did you know it was me?"

"I've been teaching here in Magic School long enough to know when students are doing what, and I've been teaching for eighty million years to be exact. Also, I called your mother and she said she's on her way, so just hang around, say your good-byes, and be off.

"Am I the only one that is leaving Magic School?" I asked.

"Why, of course not, only the student teachers and the regular teachers are staying," he replied.

I guess I won't be seeing Drake around, I thought in my mind. I went out the office and gathered the bag my clothes were in.

I went to Grace's dorm to tell her I was leaving, but it seemed she was still asleep.

I went out of her room and went to Drake's dorm. Thankfully, he was awake. His room was slightly bigger than all the other students' dorms. He had a brown old-fashioned desk with paper and junk all over it. He was sitting in his desk, going through the papers. Then he noticed that I was at his door.

"Max, what are you doing up this early?" he asked me worriedly.

"I was just about to ask you the same thing," I replied while I laughed a little.

"I do this every day and prepare for the class I'm going to teach," he replied.

"Well, I'm leaving, and Mom is coming to pick me up to go back to school," I said.

"I'm sorry I can't come home with you and Mom, but Magic School's priorities are kind of more important, but I can come on holidays," Drake said sadly.

"It's okay," I said. No! It is not! I haven't seen you in eight years, and you want to stay at Magic School, I said in my head.

"Uh, bye, Drake," I said with a smile.

"Bye, bro," he replied.

The next dorm I went to was Jonah's. His was probably hard to find, but I found it anyway. I tried to open the door, but it was locked.

Then Vincent opened the door and said, "Max," in surprise. I went in the room and said, "I'm leaving."

Jonah was on the floor, meditating, then Vincent pushed him, and he fell. "What is it!" Jonah yelled at Vincent.

"Max is leaving," Vincent said back.

Jonah looked at me and stood up. "Max, it was nice to meet you," Jonah said as we shook hands.

After I said good-bye to everybody except for Cindy—because she was in trouble—there was a door slam.

"That must be my mom," I said as I left the room. When I was in the main hall, I saw my mother. "Max!" she yelled.

She ran toward me with her arms wide out. She gave me a big hug and lifted me up. "I'm glad you're alive!" she yelled.

"Why wouldn't I?" I said, smiling with my teeth showing, feeling awkward.

"Do you have your stuff ready?" she said.

"Yeah, there, right there." I pointed.

"Where's Drake?" she asked me.

Drake opened his door, and he ran to our mom. She kissed him and asked him, "How are things going?"

Then Chiron came out of his office and said, "Mrs. Iverson, how are you doing? Max has been a big help completing one of our most dangerous missions this summer."

She looked at me and smiled.

Then I had realized that I spent my whole summer doing a mission that I could've died any moment.

Lucas and Cindy rushed out of Chiron's office. Cindy looked at me and ran and hugged me. "I'm gonna miss you," she said with no sympathy at all, but she was trying to play it off.

"See you some time." Lucas said.

My mom said, "Let's go," and we both left Magic School.

Even though I hated the missions I was assigned, I still liked Magic School and I couldn't wait until next year.

We were in the studio's parking lot, and I saw my mom's car. We entered the car and were on our way. It was about twenty minutes before we finally reached my house. It was the same flat old house. I could smell pasta, which meant that my mom cooked her famous broccoli casserole for breakfast. I threw my bag in my room, washed my hands, and went to the dining table. My mom put a lot on my plate, and I was ready to eat. In five minutes, I was done.

"So when do I start school?"

"Tomorrow," she said.

"What!" I yelled.

"I'm sorry, Max, I know that you've been working hard, but

you have already missed the first two days of school."

I drooped back to my room, and I lay down.

"Max! I'm going to work. Be good," my mom said.

I ran out of my room and said, "Since when do you go to work in the morning?"

"Since you left to go to Magic School."

"You work at night too, when am I going to see you?" I added

"Weekends, and there are some leftover biscuits and chicken in the fridge for lunch, dinner, and breakfast for tomorrow morning."

She kissed me on the cheek and said, "I love you," and she left.

I didn't know what to do for the whole day. I couldn't play outside, couldn't go to a friend's house, and couldn't watch TV all day. I thought of going to Magic School, but I just couldn't. I went into the freezer and got some ice cream. I turned the TV on and ate ice cream. After two hours of eating, I looked for the spare key so I could take a walk.

I grabbed my watch to keep track of time. Not many people were on the streets anymore. Then I heard footsteps. I was too tired and bored to wonder whether it was a monster. Suddenly, something erupted from the ground. It was a giant lion, its fur was spiky, and it had a goat arise from its spine and had a snake for a tail.

"Things can't get any weirder," I said as it pounced on toward me.

I looked for White Fang, but I had left it in my other pants that were dirty. The snake tail almost bit me. Then I remembered that the monster was called a chimera. It pounced on me again, and surprisingly, I did a perfect back flip and put my hands in fighting position.

"How are your fists going to harm me, stupid child?" the chimera said fiercely.

I looked at the nearby fire hydrant and focused my powers on it. Then it busted, squirting high levels of water at the ugly creature.

Then I used my powers to make an earthquake that shattered all the nearby windows. People were yelling, "What happened!" And I was scared that I was going to be held accountable even though I did break their windows. I managed to make a rock rope that squeezed him tightly.

I walked closer to the chimera, and I asked, "Who sent you?"

"I would die before I tell you my sender."

I made the rope squeeze tighter, then it exploded. I ran so nobody could say that I damaged his or her property.

When I got home, it was already five. Fighting that monster was a really good way to pass the time. I watched some more TV, and I went to bed at nine. The next morning was terrible. The shower was cold and the biscuits I wanted to eat were too hard. I ran to the bus stop, waiting for the city bus. I didn't take the school bus because I didn't really live near my school, so I had to wake up early every day. The bus took a lot of time before it finally came.

It took even longer to get to my school's area with all the other drop-offs. I rushed to my school and barged into my math class.

"You're late, Iverson," my math teacher said.

"I know, but—"

"Detention," he said, cutting me off.

Everybody in the class laughed at me, especially the school bully, Todd Burgawitz. He had been bullying me since second grade. Then the bell rang, and it was time for lunch. When I put my stuff in my locker, Todd showed up behind me.

"How about we take a field trip to the bathroom," Todd said. He grabbed me by the shirt and took me to the bathroom.

"What are you doing!" I yelled.

"How about a swirly," Todd yelled happily.

He dumped my head in pee. Then he ran. When I walked out of the bathroom, people laughed as I walked by. I realized I forgot to wash off. They could tell it was pee because it looked like it, and it smelled like it, plus Todd told everybody.

Luckily, I came in the second period of school, and the day

was almost over. I planned to get revenge on Todd and that meant using my powers.

When he was getting water from the water fountain, I used my powers to make the water spray on his pants to make it look like he wet himself. Later, when he used the bathroom, I used my powers to make all the toilet water unleash on Todd. His clothes were soaked in pee. Everybody laughed as hard as they could, and I was happier than I could ever be.

The last bell rang, and I forgot I had detention. I walked to my math teacher's class, and he was writing on the board.

"Max, you may go, I know what you go through, you have a reason to be late, and I just said you had detention so the other kids wouldn't say, 'That's not fair.' So you may go," he said.

I ran out that room like I was the flash. I jumped in excitement and felt like I just found out I was going to live forever.

After school that day, I couldn't wait until the next day. I thought about what I was going to do when I got home. All I cared about now was happiness, and no one could take that away from me.

Chapter 18

I Meet My "Wonderful" Father

I went outside and was waiting for the bus to arrive so I could go home. Then I saw a man in a brown detective coat with a detective hat, dark sunglasses, black pants, and church shoes. He looked at me sharply. I sat down at the nearby bench. He kept looking at me, and I decided to ignore him. He walked closer to me and said.

"Max! I need to talk to you."

"Who are you!" I yelled. "Get lost."

"Don't you recognize me?" he said again.

He took off his hat and shades, and it was Chiron.

"What! What are you doing here?" I asked. "Why couldn't you just dress like you usually do or told me who you are?"

"Didn't want any humans to see me, plus you have to say that I am a little odd looking."

"I thought the magical boundaries would prevent humans from seeing you," I replied.

"Still, don't want to take chances. Anyhow, I'm here to notify you that the gods have demanded to see you in Olympus."

Part of me was happy; the other part of me was scared because I didn't know what the gods might want me for.

"Have any idea why they want me?" I asked Chiron.

"Yes, it seemed you might have upset the god of war, Ares." Then I remembered what happened at the fishing dock.

"I'm here to take you to Olympus. Since you have angered Ares, all the gods who have sided with him are against you and want you to explain. We must get there immediately because the gods don't like to waste time."

"So where is this so-called Olympus?"

"At the very top of United Nations Headquarters," he said.

"Why is the most important location in Greek mythology located in a building?"

"Look! Once the human race started to evolve, the gods didn't have anywhere else to go, so they settled in areas around the world."

"Oh!" I replied.

Chiron pulled out a piece of chalk out of his pocket. He started to draw something on the wall.

"What are you doing?"

"Summoning a portal to where the headquarters is located."

"Why couldn't you just use a potion?"

"Because I like the old-fashioned way."

Suddenly, the drawing started to glow. It unleashed violent rays of purple light. Then in a minute, both of us disappeared. We were in a different place. But I knew we were in Manhattan.

"The building is there," he pointed. When I looked, the building was huge. It was like a glass rectangle standing up.

"Let's go, Max, we must hurry."

I ran thinking where could Olympus be if it's in a building. We entered, and the inside was like a hotel.

"So how do we get there?"

"As I have said, just follow me," he replied. He ran up the stairs.

"Can't we just take the elevator!" I yelled, but he didn't reply.

"We kept running, and after at least six minutes, I noticed that the staircase began to be gold. "Chiron! Gold, the staircases are gold!" I yelled.

"That's how you know we are close to Olympus." Suddenly, the stairs ended.

There was a black stone temple with twelve giant stone pillars holding it up. It was covered in dark clouds and black snow, which was weird. From looking at it straight, it looked small, but it was large.

"So this is Olympus," I said.

"Yes, isn't it beautiful? Chiron replied.

"How do we get in?" I asked.

"As I said before, just follow me."

He walked through the clouds, but for some reason, he didn't fall. He turned back and asked, "Are you coming?"

"Uh, yeah!" I replied.

As soon as my foot touched the cloud, I fell right through it. "Ahhhhhhhhhh!" I yelled.

When I was plunging down to who knows where, I realized that Chiron had caught me, and I was just panicking.

"Just believe that you can walk on cloud, that's the only way you can cross."

I closed my eyes and believed I could do anything. Before you knew it, I was already at the doors of Olympus along with Chiron. Chiron opened the door, and it was like a big empty city hall. The light was bright. There wasn't one spot of dimness.

"Max! Make sure to be on your best behavior with the gods."

"Don't sweat it," I replied with no problem.

"Max, this is no joke. If you make the gods angrier than they already are, they will destroy you into ash."

"There are a lot of doors here," I said, trying to change the subject.

"Come on, Max, we are almost there."

When we finally reached our destination, the door that led to the throne of the gods was gold with Greek pictures and words. I was about to open the door when Chiron slapped my hand.

"This is what I was talking about, Max. You just don't go to someone's door and open it, you knock," he said.

I knocked on the door, and it opened by itself.

"Come in!" a voice said.

I looked around and saw really big tall people sitting on golden chairs with a red carpet, which they sat on that extended to the end of the chairs. They were as tall as skyscrapers. The one in the middle had the highest chair. Suddenly, I knew which god was which. I looked at Ares, who was five seats to the right down from the one in the middle who was Zeus.

Zeus had a long gray beard and hair; wore a long ancient Greek tunic. The chair next to Zeus was empty, and I thought I knew whose throne it was—Hades. On the other side next to Zeus was a man with a short black beard and hair. He had a button shirt with a red sunrise on it and Hawaiian shorts and slippers. He had a trident in his hand, which obviously meant he was Poseidon, my father. I longed for this moment, and now I got it.

Then a voice came, "Max Iverson, you have been accused of associating with an organization that destroys gods and will be sent on trial." Suddenly, the room was dark; and Poseidon, Zeus, and Ares were sitting on high chairs while I was standing in a witness stand.

"Max, is it true that you are part of Black Hand?" Zeus asked me.

"No, sir, I replied nervously. "Ares is lying!" I shouted.

Then Zeus looked mad and summoned a lightning bolt and threw it at my witness stand. The witness stand blew up, and he yelled at me, "Don't you ever yell at me, or I will blow you to bits!"

That's when I knew what Chiron meant about not angering the gods.

"Why would Ares lie when he has better things to do," Zeus said.

"He's the god of war. He wants to start a fight between the gods and me," I replied softly.

"You have a point," Zeus replied. "I'm sorry, Ares, but we don't have enough evidence that he betrayed, so, Max Iverson, your trial is over."

"Yes!" I yelled.

When we were back in the throne, I walked out. Ares followed but now in normal size. He grabbed me by the collar and slammed me to a wall.

"This is not over, punk!" he yelled.

"Let go of me!" I said.

"I'm gonna crush you, seaweed boy."

I thought of using White Fang, but I didn't have it. I kicked him in the stomach then hit him in the face. I ran when I could.

I met up with Chiron and he asked me how the trial went.

"Quick!" I said, relieved.

"Well, your father wants to see you back in the throne alone," Chiron said. My palms started to sweat, and I went in the room.

"Haven't you ever heard of knocking?" my dad said, laughing. I looked way up, and I saw him.

"Oh! Did I forget to shrink to my small size?" he said.

Then he minimized to a regular man's figure. He patted me on the back and said, "Son, it's been a while since I've seen you. So how have things been going?"

"Fine," I replied.

"Oh! And your brother, Drake, how is he?"

"Don't really know," I replied again.

"Instead of saying I'm sorry about not being in most of your life, I'm giving you this." He held out three small seashells.

"I am not trying to sound ungrateful, but you are giving me seashells?" I asked.

"They are magic seashells that can grant you any wish you want," he replied.

"I would say that's impossible, but now anything is possible."

"I'm sure you will make the right wishes," my dad said seriously.

I took the seashells from my dad and put them in my pocket.

"I should be going now," I said.

"Wait! Can't we have something to eat or take a tour?" he asked desperately.

"Sure," I replied.

He walked me around Olympus and showed me rooms and

special places. Then I thought of why he was never in my life and why he didn't help my mom raise me. Even though I was scared to ask, I still did.

"Uh, how come you never, uh, stayed with my mom to raise me and my brother?" I said nervously. "Max, many gods fall for humans who can see magical things. It is impossible for a god to stay with a human forever. One because gods are immortal and humans will die sooner or later, and because I have certain duties that I have to attend to every day. Plus, Max, you were a mistake.

"Your mother and I never meant to have a second child, we only planned to raise one," he said.

My whole confidence and love for my father were destroyed. I stared at the ground, looking sad.

He looked at me and knew I was not happy.

"Max, I didn't mean to say what I said, you were a blessing," he added.

"No, you're just saying that to make me feel better."

"I'm sorry, son, but your mother didn't have enough money to raise a second child," he said sympathetic.

I still didn't feel better, but I said it was okay, so I didn't have to hear him say excuses about why he wasn't in my life. The reason I wasn't mad was because of what happened between Zemnas and his father Aeolus. Plus, my dad was right. A god just can't devote his life to a human and a child twenty-four-seven.

He sniffed the air and said, "The food is ready."

We walked to dining area, and it was as big as the White House. There were banquets and food sections on drinks, bakery, dessert, seafood, vegetables, and fruits.

Life as a god is sweet, I said in my mind. I rushed, got a plate, and ate my food. "You're not going to pray?" he asked me.

"I'm already in Olympus," I replied, laughing.

I ate everything on my plate, but I wasn't hungry; I was ready to go. As much as I was anxious to see my dad, this wasn't what I expected. I grabbed a napkin, wiped my mouth, and left. He ran out and followed.

"Max! If it's me, I'm sorry, but what can I do to help?"

I turned, saying to myself, why am I putting my own father through this? "Oh, it's nothing, it was just . . . it was too stuffy in there," I said, lying. He looked at me firmly, but I tried to ignore him.

"You know how I can tell you're lying?" he said.

"How?" I replied.

"You have the same look on your face that your mother has when she's sad or lying."

I managed a smirk. Then Zeus walked by.

"Why is Hades not in Olympus?" I asked my dad.

"Uh, we had some family issues, and he was the cause of it, so that's partially the reason. I can't really explain," he added. "So what's the drama about you being associated with the Black Hand?"

I looked at him seriously and asked him not to tell anyone.

"I kind've joined them a little bit because they tricked me," I explained.

"You joined them a little!" he yelled angrily.

"I'm sorry!" I yelled back.

"I'm sorry too, Max," he replied. Then Chiron ran in a rush toward me.

CHAPTER 19

CHIRON ACCLAIMS

" Max, I totally forgot about my speech today," he said. "We have to hurry."

"Bye, Dad," I said.

"Bye, Max," he replied.

"Thank you, sir," Chiron said respectfully.

He threw his potion on the wall, and a portal opened.

"I thought you liked the old-fashioned way," I said.

"There is no time, that's all," he replied.

We walked in the portal as I waved my hand toward my dad while we left.

Then we arrived at Magic School in the gym. The stages and everything was set up. Drake, Grace, Cindy, Vincent, Jonah, and Lucas were helping decorate the gym.

I went over to Drake and told him that I met our dad.

"Oh, that's great," Drake, said happily. "So how was he to you?"

"He is self-absorbed and a liar."

"Are you crazy?" Drake whispered. "The gods could hear you."

"Don't care anymore," I replied.

"What did he do?" he asked some more.

"He said I was a mistake," I said, mad.

He shrugged his shoulders. I went to Chiron and asked him what he was going to talk about.

"The traitor," he replied.

I thought real hard and tried to guess who the traitor could be. There was no one in my mind who could be the traitor, but I didn't care anymore. I was going to leave Magic School anyway.

"When does the speech start?"

"In about an hour," he replied.

"Then we have to hurry," I said.

"Don't worry, the speech decorations are almost ready," he said.

I tried to find my mom, and she was in a room with the door cracked. When I looked closely, she was talking to someone. I looked farther left, and it was my dad.

I could hear him saying, "I'm sorry, honey, for leaving you alone."

"Poseidon, it's been twelve years since we split up, why are you saying sorry now?" She asked.

"Uh, let's just say something reminded me of leaving you with the kids."

I turned and smiled, believing that my dad wasn't all that bad.

"And there's something else I want to discuss with you."

"What is it?" she asked.

"Max is more of an enemy to the gods than Kronos!" he yelled.

"I don't know what you're talking about."

"Max is Ares's target, and all the gods think he's a traitor."

"What do you want me to do about it?"

"At least talk to him."

"Sure," she replied.

Then they started to walk out the room, and I ran. I thought about the traitor and what my dad said. I thought hard who the traitor really was for a long time, and I never knew the traitor would be me.

"Max! Max!" Chiron was calling and looking for me.

I sneaked my way around him so my parents wouldn't see me, and I was in the gym. I didn't know whether my eyes were playing tricks on me but, I could swear that the gym was filled to the brim. I could see gods and their human spouses.

Then Chiron came back and asked me where I was.

"Uh, I was right here the whole time," I said nervously.

"Anyway, the speech is almost ready, and I need some well-known students to stand at the stage."

"Oh! I'll be on the stage in a second I need to—"

Then he cut me off, saying, "No, you need to get on the stage now. Drake, Grace, Vincent, Cindy, and Jonah were already on the stage.

In the crowd, I saw Ezinna and Felix sitting in the front row. I ran upstairs beside Drake and started to whisper to him, "How long do you think the speech will last?"

"Looking from this crowd, I would say two hours."

"We have to stand here that long?" I asked.

"If you don't want to make Chiron look stupid," he replied. When everybody was settled, Chiron started to speak.

"Good evening, ladies and gentlemen. Today, I will be discussing about certain matters that are really important. First things first, I would like to thank a king named Ezinna for letting us use his estate when we need it. He and his son have been very loyal as well. Ezinna and his son, Felix, are present here with us today. Another main thing I would like to discuss about is the traitor. Whoever the traitor is, we must find him quickly before things really get out of hand. The traitor has managed to destroy Magic School's magical boundaries and let monsters in. If anybody is associated with or knows whom the traitor is, fess up. And if I find out who knows, I will have them executed."

I gulped.

"Also, if the traitor is found, they will be sent somewhere that is worse than execution. They will be sent to Tartarus to stay there all eternity and nobody wants that."

"What is Tartarus?" I asked. I already knew, but I wanted

Drake's explanation.

"Tartarus is the Greek hell. It is beneath the underworld and is cold and sorrowful. It is full of despair. Anyone who goes there would be tortured by the Titan Kronos because he was the first one to go there."

"Wow!" I said.

"Another matter I would like to talk about is an organization called the Black Hand. They are dangerous and deadly. They have already made their moves, so we have to be cautious. Anyway, this speech is about honor and the traitor. An honorable person would tell us who the traitor was. They would report them immediately."

Drake stood up, smiled, and announced, "Look, I'm tired of listening to all this nonsense about the traitor. I got a confession to make. I'm the traitor!"

"Drake, we don't have time for foolishness, so may you please shut up and sit down," Chiron directed.

"What are you doing?" I whispered.

"I'm sorry, Max, but I really am the traitor," Drake said, smiling. He's just kidding, I said in my mind.

"You shut up!" Drake cut off Chiron.

Drake pulled out his sword viciously. He swiftly zigzagged and attacked Chiron.

Jonah took out his knife and transformed it into a spear and counteracted Drake's blow. The impact was too much.

"Drake, what are you doing!" Jonah and Chiron yelled.

"I told you, I'm the traitor!" He smiled while he yelled. "I know you gonna ask why, and it is because my stupid father abandoned me! I destroyed the magical boundaries and unleashed the monsters inside Magic School. I serve under my master, Kronos, and no one can stop me!" he boasted wickedly.

Jonah and Vincent engaged combat with Drake and then Grace joined the fight. Lucas came out of the stands and joined the fight. Then all my friends started to fight Drake. I just looked and was devastated to find out that my own brother was the traitor. I looked at my mom in the crowd and she cried. I saw Clair look confused, still sitting as if nothing was happening. Ezinna and Felix looked truly scared and in shock.

My dad rose up and yelled, "There's no way my son is a traitor!" Surprisingly, Drake fought everybody off.

He got everybody to the ground and said, "It was fun playing with you guys, but I have to go."

Then he threw a potion that blew up and sent the whole gym flying. He disappeared with the smoke.

All the demigods were lying on the floor, injured. The humans were badly hurt, including my mom. And as usual, the gods were fine. My friends and I were the ones who got hurt the most since we were at close range.

Two hours later, medic demigods and Apollo were treating the injured people. Even though I was injured, I got out of bed but sad. Then I thought back to when Ron and Barbus hinted that the traitor was "someone you trust the most," and we did not know it was Drake. I thought about it further. Maybe that was why Drake kept intercepting our attempts to contact Chiron.

I then limped to where my mom, dad, and Chiron were talking. "How could my son be a traitor?" my dad yelled.

My mom cried and cried. "I don't know what I did to let my son do these kinds of things," my mom sobbed.

"In fact, Drake was one of our best students," Chiron complained. "But why would he betray everybody? He loved Magic School and everybody in it."

I limped to my dad and mom. Then I was about to fall, but Chiron caught me. "Max, you should go get some more rest. That blast was pretty bad," he said.

I went back to my bed and slept. Before you knew it, all the human parents except for my mom were already gone, and only the gods and half bloods remained. When I got out of bed, Jonah came to me and said sorry.

"It's okay, it's not like he died or anything," I said, trying not to sound sympathetic. But deep inside, I was really sad. Cindy and Vincent came toward me and said the same thing.

Then Poseidon looked at me firmly. "I'm sorry for making it

seem like you were the traitor," he apologized.

"No problem," I said. But there was a problem, my brother was a traitor.

I went to Chiron to see what was going on, but other half bloods where swarming around him. I waited a couple of minutes before everybody left.

"Oh, good! Chiron, could I have a minute?"

"Uh! Sure, but make it quick," he replied.

"So what do we do next?"

"All the students are leaving, including Vincent and Grace because of what happened, and also Magic School will shut down momentarily, but don't worry."

"When do we leave?" I added.

"Whenever the parents decide, Max, but I know your mother would want you home." I ran to find my friends, and they were in the gym.

"You leaving yet, Max?" Jonah asked me.

"No, not yet, what about you all?"

"We don't know, but we packed our things," Cindy replied.

Vincent walked to me and patted me on the back and said, "I don't know what it feels like, but if my brother were a traitor, I would find him and kill him."

"Vincent, shut up!" Cindy whispered.

I shrugged it off, acting like I didn't hear anything, and I walked away. Then Cindy ran after me, worried.

CHAPTER 20

I SAY GOOD-BYE TO SOME GOOD
FRIENDS

"Wait, Max!" Cindy yelled.

"What is it?" I asked as I turned around.

"Sorry for Vincent's outburst, it's just that we are worried."

"Why does everybody think I'm sad!" I yelled. She tried to place her hand on my shoulder, but I moved away.

"My brother's treachery was unexpected. No one would've thought that he was a traitor, but he fooled us all. I loved him a lot, but he betrayed everyone, and anyone who betrays people are not human beings."

"Anyway, Max, next year there will be a lot more half bloods that will attend Magic School."

"Why are you telling me this?" I asked.

"Because Chiron said since Drake is gone, no one can fill his slot as a swordsman teacher. Also Chiron wants more classes for certain people to teach it."

"Let me guess, I was selected."

"Uh, all of us were," she replied happy.

"What?" I asked again.

"Chiron liked our performance in our last mission, so he's putting us in charge of the new classes." I managed to smile even

176

with what was going on.

"Come on, Max, let's go back to the gym," she said.

"Sure," I replied.

For some reason, I was happy again. When I got back to the gym, I saw Chiron and my friends talking. Chiron turned and saw us.

"Oh, good, all of you are here," he said.

"What is it, Master Chiron?" Cindy asked.

Chiron started to talk. "Now listen. All of you must report and be at Magic School next June. There is an important mission you must undertake. Kronos wants to resurrect himself using an object called the Sapphire of Dreams, we must locate and secure it.

"The prediction is that Kronos will use the object to resurrect himself if his servants get their hands on it. As soon as he's resurrected, he will alter the balance of the earth's electromagnetic fields. This would have the effect of damaging the ozone layers and the ecosystem. It would also cause asteroids to land on earth to destroy it. The earth would then not be able to support life, and the human race would become extinct.

"The Black Hand also wants to kill all the gods to be in power, and they must be stopped too. I will give you more details at the meeting of June. You must train and be prepared. It is the right thing to do."

"It is—," I tried to say something.

And he said to me, "Bye. Max, and bye to your friends." Then he walked off and my friends were awing in suspense.

"He didn't even wait for anybody to say something back to him to know more," I grumbled. This mission just finished, and all of a sudden, there is another mission, I said to myself.

In my mind, I was mad because I would spend the whole summer doing the same thing, but I didn't let my friends know what I was thinking. And it was not easy to object to Chiron.

"What is it, Max?" Jonah asked.

"Another mission," Cindy said lazily.

"It can't be," Vincent added.

"Unfortunately," I said, "we all have to spend the summer kicking monsters' butts."

"That's not so bad. Where is the mission?" Vincent said excited.

"Well, obviously, he didn't say. He didn't give details," I said as if Vincent didn't hear a word Chiron said. "He said that all of us must report back to Magic School next June for more instructions about the mission. Vincent, got it?"

"Yeah, thanks." I had a feeling when Chiron was talking Vincent was daydreaming about the next mission.

"Okay! We got it, I'll go to Boston," Cindy said.

"My flight to Africa is midnight," Jonah announced. "But first, I must stop in Europe, then Johannesburg for the finals of the FIFA World Soccer Cup, then Lagos, and finally, to my village."

"That is a long trip," Clair stated. "And for me, I will go off in the morning to good old San Francisco."

"I am not going anywhere. I have to stay in crummy old New York. I have to go live with my grandma in Bronx since I'm not allowed to stay in Magic School because of the incident," Vincent announced. "Max, where you going?"

"Well, I guess I'll go back to my middle school," I told them.

Immediately, they all left to the entrance of Magic School, except Cindy, all with one thing in mind—the next mission in June.

"Let's go," I told Cindy.

I walked and fidgeted around, waiting for my ride while Cindy was playing some stupid game on her laptop.

I thought about what Chiron said. I knew it was going to bother me. I knew those dreams would come again, but most importantly, for some reason, I kept thinking about the evil Black Hand and the object we must recover to stop Kronos from resurrecting himself.

Then in about ten minutes, my mom came.

I didn't even hear her weeping behind me until I heard her scream, "Why are you standing there? Aren't you ready to go?"

Then I turned and asked her where the car was. She walked

passed me and opened the entrance of Magic School.

"Bye, guys," I said as I left.

We entered the car, and I literally passed out into sleep or rather a "coma." I was really tired. I didn't say a word to my mom until we got home.

But there was a feeling I had when I slept.

I had a feeling that I was gonna see Drake again; but the next time, it wouldn't be pleasant. I was totally stressed—and worn-out. Suddenly, I thought of my friends and how much I cared for them. I wanted to see them so bad, and suddenly, I was in Magic School again. This time, my body was hollow. I looked at my skin and touched myself to see whether I was dreaming.

Then Cindy saw me and shouted, "Max! Is that you? I thought you left!"

"Well, I did, but I was thinking about coming back to Magic School, and here I am."

Cindy closed her eyes and scratched her head. "Oh, I know what it is called," Cindy said, excited. "It's called astral projection. You just think about something, and your spirit is where you want to be, live. You can walk and talk and people can see you."

"So where is my body?" I said, worried.

"Wherever you left it, silly," she said.

"Bye, Cindy, and thanks for cheering me up," I said.

"No problem," she replied.

Then I thought of getting back in my body, and there I was. I opened my eyes, and we were close to home. Ten minutes later, we were home.

"Max, get out of the car," my mom said urgently.

I got up and got out of the car. For once, I was glad to see my house. I remembered my brother, Drake, and when we were kids. He used to take me for a walk. At that moment, I wasn't sad. I was actually proud. As I walked in my house, I had my head held high, knowing that next year's mission was going to be a breeze. Especially, when I would be back, better than ever, with my newly discovered powers, and I felt nothing could stop me.

www.ingramcontent.com/pod-product-compliance
Lightning Source LLC
Chambersburg PA
CBHW050533190726
48284CB00003B/1056